J. T. PETTY

Clemency Pogue

The Scrivener Bees

ILLUSTRATED BY DAVID MICHAEL FRIEND

SIMON AND SCHUSTER

SIMON AND SCHUSTER
First published in Great Britain in 2007 by Simon & Schuster UK Ltd
Africa House, 64-78 Kingsway, London WC2B 6AH
A CBS COMPANY

Originally published in 2007 by Simon & Schuster Books for Young Readers,
An imprint of Simon & Schuster Children's Publishing Division, New York

A CIP catalogue record for this book is available from the British Library.

ISBN: 978-1-8473-8017-3

1 3 5 7 9 10 8 6 4 2

Printed and bound in Great Britain by Cox & Wyman Ltd, Reading, Berks

www.simonsays.co.uk

For my family

Also by J.T. Petty

Clemency Pogue: Fairy Killer
Clemency Pogue: The Hobgoblin Proxy

Clemency Pogue

PROLOGUE

Motherless children have a hard time. Worse than that, they don't even have their mothers around to blame for it.

Inky Mess very much wanted someone to blame.

"Where's your mother?" he asked the nearest goblin.

"Motherrrrr . . ." The scrawny creature gargled the word like spoiled milk, spat it on the tunnel floor, and ground it under hoof.

"Don't any of you have mothers?" Inky asked.

The goblins crowding around him scowled and hissed and shook their heads.

Inky smiled.

"Tell me again about the Leviathans," he said.

"Leviathannn . . . ," growled a goblin.

"And the Forgetting Book." Inky riffled through his journal, a ramshackle stack of dog-eared loose-leaf covered in pencil markings.

"You said I could use it to control the Make-Believe."

"Forgetting Book," tittered a goblin.

"Leviathan Ink in the Forgetting Book," whispered another. Over a dozen of the creatures crouched in a rough circle around Inky, watching the boy with doglike admiration.

"The Forgetting Book makes the Make-Believe believe," said yet another.

Inky pulled the pencil from behind his ear and touched the point to the tip of his tongue, already well blackened by graphite. As he had done for months now, Inky Mess listened to the sound and idiot flurry of goblin voices, trying to pull meaning from the chaos.

"Tallygob. Terrible Tallygob hob and terrible fairy," a goblin said.

"The Tallygob . . . ," Inky said, riffling through his journal to an entry, penciled in his own precise handwriting: " . . . a *creature called the* Tallygob . . . *keeper of the* Forgetting Book."

"I want the Forgetting Book," Inky said. "How do I get it?"

The goblins shifted and muttered, pulling

anxiously at their long ears, some tangling them bonnet-like under their chins in nervous knots.

"How do I get the Forgetting Book?" Inky asked more forcefully.

"Imp . . . imp . . . ," a goblin stuttered.

"Ossible," another tried.

"Impossible. Terrible fairy, Lost and Forgotten."

Inky flipped through his journal until he found, " . . . *Tallygob uses some fairy to guard the Forgetting Book.*"

"Nothing's impossible. How do I get the book?" Inky asked.

"Don't know," whispered a goblin. "Impossible."

"I want answers!" Inky said, shaking his journal at the goblins, who shied from the rustling pages.

"Sss . . . Sss . . ." The stuttering goblin's chin shook as it forced out the word "Ssssscrivener."

The other goblins fell silent. Inky looked at the stutterer.

"Scrivener," the goblin said again. "Bees."

"Scrivener! Scrivener! Scrivener Bees!"

the other goblins chorused, pressing in on Inky with shining eyes.

Inky flipped to the section of his journal where he had already begun his study of these Scrivener Bees. At the top of the page he had written, "*Scrivener, (noun) One who writes. A scribe.*"

Inky licked the tip of his pencil and added below, "*The Scrivener Bees are my answer.*"

"What Scrivener Bees do, they tattoo truth!" a goblin screeched.

"The Scrivener Bees," Inky said. "Where do I find them?"

The goblin chorus fell silent.

"The Vale of the Kettlepot Blossoms," one whispered.

"Hidden," said another.

"Ssss . . . sssecret. No gob knows."

"The Kettlepot Blossoms . . . ," Inky mused, tapping the tip of the pencil against his teeth. A "vale" could be a valley, or any kind of forested hollow. If he could discover this vale, the Scrivener Bees would have his answers, and soon Inky would have the Forgetting Book.

"I'll find it," he said.

CHAPTER 1

Clemency Pogue realized that the closest her parents came to each other was kissing her opposite cheeks at the same time. She kept trying to duck out of the way at the last moment and trick them into a little affection.

"Clem dear, do you want a kiss good night or not?" her mother asked, eyes ringed with fatigue after a full day of work.

"Yes, please," Clemency said. Mr. and Mrs. Pogue leaned down to the bed with puckered lips. Clemency feinted forward and then dodged back, leaving a head-sized gap of empty space between her parents' kissers. Mr. and Mrs. Pogue stopped in midair, lips unpuckering.

"Rascal," her father said, tousling Clem's hair. "Sleep well. I love you."

"I love you," her mother said to Clemency.

Then Mr. and Mrs. Pogue looked at each other and sighed. It was less the kind of sigh you would expect from turtledoves and more the kind of sigh you'd expect from leaky tires.

"I love you," Clemency said to them both, hoping it was catching.

Clemency had stayed up most of the night before, madly scheming ways to make her parents fall back in love. She had come up with a plan involving two mop-heads, rubber cement, a bag of chowder, some string, and a hobgoblin. But she knew that it was not her right to call on the hobgoblin Chaphesmeeso unless a truly earth-shattering catastrophe was at hand, especially with the fugitive changeling still at large.

But it frustrated her enormously to be faced with a problem she could not smash. She was Clemency Pogue! She had traveled the world! Twice! In pants of her own design! Vanquished dangers most could not imagine! And invented root beer in her spare time!

Yet she could not make her parents be nice to each other. Sleep would not be denied a second night and was pressing hard on Clemency's eyelids with dry, cottony fingers.

But as she drifted off, Clemency's thoughts took a working vacation to Brazil. She remembered a hopeless and love-struck boy she had helped there. Clem had returned to life the Fairy of Love and Tenderness, by the discovery of the dead sprite's name.

"Twittamore," she whispered. The fairy could help her; she would have to, because Clemency knew her name. Just before sleep enveloped her, Clemency said, "Twittamore, come away to me."

Clemency woke at dawn to the muted whirr of fairy wings.

Near the window, the Fairy of Love and Tenderness used her wand to touch a fat, grundy housefly, and then pointed at a spider's web in the corner of the room.

The fly's segmented vision became a collage of interlocking hearts, and giddy with affection, he charged the web. In the eyes of the fly, the spider was suddenly gorgeous, playful, each of those eight legs going *all* the way up.

"My dearest! My immortal beloved!" buzzed the fly as he tangled himself in the spider's web.

The spider loved the fly, much like the author loves pancakes. In a matter of moments, the fly was cocooned and several hours early for a lunch date.

Clemency watched the fairy swiftly send two more houseflies to rose-colored doom before she heard her parents' muffled voices from the kitchen.

"Twittamore," Clem said. The fairy's attention snapped to her like a sticky stone.

Clemency crept to her door and eased it open a mite. Through the narrow gap, she watched her dad pour batter into a waffle iron as her mom gathered her things for work.

"Not this year, we can't afford it," her mom said.

"It's only once that you'll turn forty," her father said. "We should celebrate it."

"Fine, celebrate! Celebrate all you want, I'll be at work. One of us has to make a living."

"Now, honey . . ."

"Honey your waffles. Don't 'honey' me."

Clemency grimaced at the fairy, who was hovering by her head.

"That's my mom and dad," she said softly. "I want them to be nice to each other."

"Don't yell, you'll wake Clemency," her

"Honey your waffles. Don't 'honey' me."

father said, throttling his wooden waffle-mixing spoon.

"I'm going to work," her mother said.

"We should do something nice for your birthday," her father muttered sullenly.

"Twittamore," Clemency whispered solemnly, "make my mom and dad love each other again."

The fairy nodded and buzzed into the kitchen.

"You want to get me something nice, get yourself a job." Mrs. Pogue threw her satchel over her shoulder and headed for the door. Twittamore hovered midway between Mr. and Mrs. Pogue, looking from one to the other. Clemency's mom slammed out the door while her dad snarled and attacked the waffle batter with his spoon.

The fairy turned and darted back into Clemency's room. Clemency eased the door shut.

"So?" she said.

The fairy flew to Clem's ear.

"It's too late," the fairy whispered.

"What?" Clemency exclaimed.

"They already love each other."

The Journal of Inky Mess, Excerpt 1

Day and night means nothing down here, so I won't even try to guess the date. But I've been with the goblins for months now at least. I'm learning what I can from them, but it's not easy. They talk in idiotic circles, riddles that aren't. If I could find the <u>Scrivener Bees</u>, I could get my answers.

GOBLINS

They've taken me as one of their own, or, even more, they've taken me as their leader even though they're hard to control and utterly stupid but they love . . . respect . . . admire . . . follow me, they follow me around like a row of ducks. None of them have names, which is important down here and may be the biggest difference between goblins and hobgoblins (other than those ridiculous hats and the fact that hobgoblins tend to be fat as hogs), but anything in the Make-Believe with a name can be <u>controlled</u>. Hobgoblins have names, and fairies have names, and all of them are recorded in <u>The Forgetting Book</u>. The Forgetting Book is key; I must get my hands on it.

HOBGOBLINS

Hobgoblins would be harmless, if it wasn't for fairies. Hobgoblins seem to be the "brains" of the Make-Believe, but the brains in headcheese don't necessarily make it smart. Hobgoblins and fairies are the authority down here, and the hobgoblins take their orders from a creature called the Tallygob. He's the oldest of the hobgoblins, and keeper of the Forgetting Book.

The goblins hate hobgoblins and fear fairies. It was the hobgoblins and fairies that were trying to kill me. The fairies are still coming after me. I've had to stay vigilant not to end up dead at the end of a wand.

CHANGELINGS

I am a changeling. I've watched the goblins make changelings out of clay that smells like salt and is faintly fishy. I am made of clay and Leviathan Ink. The goblins won't say much about Leviathan Ink except that it comes from Leviathans (duh). I am made of clay. I am made of clay.

SHARON RIVER MENTAL HOSPITAL

The place they took my mother when she went mad. I shouldn't call her my mother—she is not—and she did not go mad, she only recognized me for what I was. But **Sharon River** is where they took my mother. The goblins helped me steal a phone book and I found the address for the hospital, and when I was reading, it made the goblins tremble before me like frightened mice, like they thought reading it was magic, dangerous magic. Is that what <u>Human Magic</u> is? It makes sense . . . the goblins say the **Scrivener** Bees use "human magic," and a scrivener is somebody who writes. . . .

CHAPTER 2

The night guard at the Sharon River Asylum saw nothing but empty shadows where Inky's escort of goblins stood. A dozen of the creatures waited around his desk, giggling and scratching at their scrawny bottoms.

"Sleep," whispered one.

"Drowsy-making lullaby," said another.

"Sleep-a-bye. Dream-a-bye. Good-a-bye. Good-a-night."

Inky watched from in secret, the deep purple splotches on his face camouflaging him more fully in the shadows. He had watched and wondered at the work of goblin whispers many times now. The whispers had no effect on children, but drowsy adults could be lulled into sleep by goblin voices, and sleeping adults could be near-hypnotized by the same. Perhaps it was because dreams were as close to childhood as adults would allow themselves to get.

The night guard's chin dropped slowly to his chest.

"Nightmare crawlies, underskin beetles," whispered a goblin into his ear, infecting his sleep with nightmares.

Inky crept forward. The goblins were already pressed against the barred door behind the guard's desk, arms and legs straining through the gaps like spiders caught in a drain.

The topmost drawer in the desk held a patient directory. Inky flipped through it until he found "Mess, Madeleine."

"Mom," he said softly. The file noted the dozens of pills and shots she was to be given daily. There was a space to record all of the visitors she had received, but it was empty. Neither Inky's dad nor his brother, Gilbert, had come in years. The bottom of the file gave Madeleine Mess's bed number, in the Catatonic Ward.

Ahead, the goblins hissed and grunted in frustration, shaking the iron door.

Inky lifted the keys from the guard's belt and pushed his way silently through the goblins. Careful not to jangle the keys, Inky unlocked the door and swung it open.

"Clever, clever Inky," a goblin said.

He led the goblins down the empty, moonlit hallway.

"Catatonic Ward," he read aloud. The words were written above the large swinging doors.

"Catatonic," a goblin echoed with a grin, savoring the rhythm of the word.

"It means her brain is broken, she can't wake up."

"Catatonic, catatonic," the goblins gleefully whispered.

Some of them had their eyes closed, and some of them had their eyes open, but all of the women in the Catatonic Ward were asleep.

Inky stood with his own eyes closed before the bed of a woman as waxy and pale as a peeled potato. She looked nothing like the warm, strong mother Inky had studied in the photographs taken before his birth.

No, he silently corrected himself, his *making.* He was not *born,* he was *made.* Goblins had shaped him out of clay.

He took a ragged breath, opened his eyes, and met the vacant stare of Madeleine Mess.

Her eyes were open, and pointed at Inky, but she could not see him. If she had a mind, it was somewhere far away, playing solitaire.

"Mom?" Inky said.

There was no reaction from Madeleine. Her chest gently rose and fell with her breathing. The goblins surrounded her bed entirely, their fingers hovering inches from her nightgown.

"Mom," Inky said, more forcefully.

"Catatonic," whispered a goblin, his sickly shiny teeth like a sickle in the moonlit ward.

Inky exhaled and felt something pass out of him. A terrible calm took its place, dark and heavy like long-swollen storm clouds. This was not his mother at all.

"Catatonic," whispered another goblin.

"Catatonic, catatonic." Their voices were brittle like wind through dead leaves, their smiles sly and wicked. The word "catatonic" spread into a forest of noise around Inky.

"That's not my mom." He grinned like a goblin.

CHAPTER 3

Clemency began to think of her parents as a couple of sharp-beaked turtles, morosely crawling around, emerging from their shells every once in a while to snap at each other.

Spring had sprung, and all the children at Clemency's school were under the wands of the Fairies of Wandering Attention, Giddy Crushes, and Window Gazing.

But Clem needed no fairy charm to pass full days without hearing a single word her teacher spoke. She was thinking about her parents, and how they could possibly love each other without *liking* each other.

She had begun to worry that she was somehow responsible.

She was so distracted that she didn't even notice the Fairy of Impending Doom slowly tracing a halo in the air above her head.

Walking helped her think, and she took a meandering path home, letting the rhythmic rasp of her burlap pants ease her mind into memory.

All around her, the forest was filled with critters in the full swing of the season, taking a much simpler approach to love than Clem's mom and dad. Squirrels tumbling acrobatically together through the branches chittered affectionately. Birds perched in the thick foliage above serenaded one another with elaborately tweeted songs. Worms curled themselves into cartoon hearts and hoped that other worms would notice before the birds did. Phlegm gurgled in harsh, rasping windpipes that whispered and giggled with malice.

Clemency stopped. The voices were the same as those she had heard deep inside the earth months before. The voices of chaos, of wickedness, of baby thievery. The voices of goblins.

She turned from the path and into the trees.

"*. . . Assfrasas . . . Root beer roots . . . safrafrass . . . houndsnake juice.*" The goblin whispers resolved into words as Clemency crept deeper into the thick undergrowth.

"Frassassassas," said a goblin.

Sassafras, Clemency thought, as the sweet,

spicy odor reached her nose. There was a glen crowded with the roots just steps ahead. Clemency pushed as quietly as she could to its edge, having the distinct sensation of being a mouse pushing through a cat's whiskers.

"Asrafrafrassa." A goblin giggled.

A breeze stirred the clearing as Clemency's face broke through the undergrowth. The plants rustled, and the glen was empty.

The goblins were gone; and they had taken half of the sassafras roots with them. The glen had been plucked and churned, plants lying on their sides, roots ripped from the stem.

"The boxer-dog tails," Clemency whispered. Sassafras could be used to make root beer. The tails she had kept briefly as pets would eat nothing but root beer. Inky Mess, the changeling, had stolen the tails. Maybe the goblins were picking sassafras to feed Inky's tails. . . .

"The goblins are working for Inky Mess!" Clemency said aloud. For the rest of her walk home, the worries about her parents were pushed to a back burner while the danger posed by the fugitive changeling simmered on the fore.

She thought back to all she knew of Inky Mess. He was a *changeling*, a baby cunningly shaped from clay and left as a decoy in the cradle of a real baby stolen by goblins. Inky should have washed away with the water of his first bath, but somehow survived and grew. And now, according to the hobgoblin Chaphesmeeso, Inky posed a great danger to the Make-Believe.

In the few hours Clemency had spent with Inky, he had seemed ambitious and remarkably sharp, but not so much more wicked than most of the eleven-year-old boys she knew. How he could possibly put an end to the Make-Believe . . .

Clemency's musings were quashed as soon as she opened the door to her home. Her mom and dad seemed to be engaged in the world's most antagonistic game of charades. Mrs. Pogue was either pantomiming or fighting an invisible octopus. Mr. Pogue was covering his eyes and shaking his head.

"Clemency!" they both shouted in unison when they saw her, then glared at each other.

"What's going on?" Clemency asked.

"The silent . . ." Again, they both spoke at once, and both strangled their words midway and glared at the other for the interruption.

Clemency waited for them to try again.

"The si . . ." It happened a third time.

"Is this the silent treatment?" Clemency asked.

They nodded in unison. Clemency sighed.

GOBLINS AND HOBGOBLINS

Goblins and hobgoblins both were once children! It took me longer than it should have to figure out but I've got it now. The Forgetting Book <u>turns children into goblins</u>. I must get my hands on it, I must, I must. I don't think goblins ever die, but I'm not sure. . . . In the cavern underground where we're making our camp, I saw one of the goblins fall from a ledge what must have been a quarter mile high and land on a stalagmite, and only say "ouches and curses" and crawl away giggling. They certainly get older, and uglier, though I wouldn't call what they do "growing up," not by a long shot, and thank goodness.

THE FORGETTING BOOK

A goblin told me that the book has "pages to always," and that it "gobbles secret hobgoblin names." They are in awe of it, and they fear the Tallygob, but maybe less than they respect me. I don't think the goblins were ever clever enough to work together until I came along; never before did they realize that they could be strong. Together, I think we can take the book.

THE FORGETTING BOOK (CONTINUED)

<u>Important</u>—The Tallygob uses some fairy to guard the Forgetting Book. When I ask what the fairy does, the goblins only say, "Lost and forgotten, lost and forgotten, lost and forgotten." I try not to let the goblins' fear infect me, but sometimes . . .

FAIRIES

On the brighter side—the fairy-trap jars work! Thirty-seven fairies in my collection now, and more to come I'm sure because it's like the fairies are hunting for me, they each have a different specialty and each try to use it against me. One afflicted me with a near-fatal case of clumsiness, another gave me hiccups that almost bent me in half, the worst of them almost turned me inside out with tickling.

I've been experimenting. The legends and fairy tales from the library have all sorts of rules about fairies and I've been testing them out on my captives.

Lead has no effect on them that I can see, and neither does salt. I wonder if the fairies have read *PETER PAN*, because it freaks them out when I say, "I don't believe in fairies," though it doesn't seem to have an effect.

An important discovery! The marks on their knuckles are names! How could I have been so stupid not to figure it out sooner! I can only see the letters, and just barely, by using a magnifying glass, but they are very definitely names. And true to the stories like *RUMPELSTILTSKIN*, the fairies can be controlled by their names. But their magic is limited, I've only been able to get them to obey within their specific abilities. For example, I can make them sit, or spin, or pinch themselves, or I can make the hiccup-inducing fairy give one of my goblins hiccups, but I can't make her conjure a pile of gold or make a grilled cheese sandwich (though there seems to be a fairy for everything in the world, so perhaps there is a fairy of golden grilled cheese sandwiches out there).

Important discovery number two! I've figured out how to kill the fairies: by the rules set out in *PETER PAN AND WENDY*! The very first fairy I caught after coming underground, the alligator-green fairy who tried to kill me in a way I'm too embarrassed to even write down, her name is Spankynick, and all it took was my saying "I don't believe in Spankynick" for her to spin inside her jar and drop dead! When I said, "I do believe in Spankynick," she popped back up as if from a light nap, like nothing had happened. I spent hours killing fairies and bringing them back to life again. Good times.

I've been trying to teach the goblins how to use the fairy-trap jars, but they're not so clever as the children they once were. And there are too many fairies for me to trap them all myself. I need a plan. Scheme, scheme, scheme . . .

CHAPTER 4

Much to Clemency's chagrin, her parents found a loophole in their silent treatment.

"Could you tell your mother that she doesn't have to make such a show of disliking the soup?" her father said.

"Tell your father that I'm too tired to talk about this right now."

"Tell your mother that unless she can tell you to tell me what I told you to tell her that upset her, then you'll have to tell her that I can't tell you to apologize to her for me."

Clemency considered hiding under her soup bowl.

She went to bed early and put her pillow over her head in the hope that she wouldn't be able to hear her mom and dad arguing. They had lost all pretense of the silent treatment.

"What do you want me to say?" came her dad's muffled voice through the door and the goose down.

"What do *you* want *me* to say?" said her muffled mom.

"What do *you* want *me* to say!" They batted the phrase back and forth until they had beaten the question mark into an exclamation point.

Clemency added one more to her list of impossible achievements by managing to fall asleep despite the racket.

The shouting she could sleep through, but the harsh whispers wriggling in from the kitchen yanked Clemency from sleep like centipedes nibbling in her ears.

Goblins.

Clemency's bare feet lowered silently to the floor.

Through the crack in her door, she saw a withered goblin, the color of ash in midnight's moonlight, straining to reach the sassafras hanging to dry over the stove.

Clemency eased her door open and saw two more goblins giggling near the door to her mom and dad's room.

Clemency's eyes widened. She needed to defend her home; she needed a weapon.

"Safrafrassa!"

She called the knobby piece of maple leaning next to the front door her "walking stick," but knew that it could as easily be called a "jabbing," "clobbering," or, in this case, "goblin-bludgeoning stick."

She eased out of her room as the two other goblins lifted their comrade so that he could reach the drying roots above the stove.

"Safrafrassa!" he whispered.

Clemency crouched low and eased around her dad's ottoman. Her goblin-bludgeoning stick was less than five steps away, a short dash past the sofa.

The topmost goblin snatched a handful of sassafras and all three tumbled softly to the floor.

Now was Clemency's chance. She tensed to spring, slipped around the arm of the sofa, and froze. Her dad's sleeping breath rustled her bangs.

He was sleeping on the sofa.

Clemency's breath caught in her throat. As far as she knew, this was the first time in her life that her parents had not slept in the same bed.

She glanced back at her parents' bedroom

and saw, through the open door, two goblins crawl stealthily away from the bed where her mother was soundly sleeping.

Fear and confusion played tetherball with her brain. The goblins . . . Her mother . . . Her parents . . .

Before Clemency could react, the two goblins had joined the three by the kitchen stove and all five spilled noiselessly out through the front door and into the night.

Clemency looked through the front window, but the goblins were already underground and away. She picked up a half-dried sassafras root off the kitchen floor.

What had the goblins done to her parents? Was goblin meddling responsible for their crumbling marriage? A small hope shone through Clemency's fear. If goblins were to blame for her parents' troubles, then maybe there was something she could do about it.

Clemency walked into the bedroom where her mom was peacefully sleeping. There seemed to be nothing wrong.

"Mom," she said.

One of her mom's eyes opened.

"Clemency?"

"Are you all right, Mom?"

Her mom inhaled and opened her other eye.

"Of course, honey," she said. "Everything's fine. Your dad's just . . . Everything's fine."

Clemency looked at her dubiously.

"Go back to sleep, honey."

Fat chance of that.

"Chaphesmeeso," she said, "come away to me."

The moonlit garden behind the house was unnaturally quiet, the trees at the edge of the Pogue property a dark wall like a chorus line of reapers.

"Chaphesmeeso," Clemency whispered again, listening nervously for the goblins' return.

A soft geyser of earth erupted back among the trees.

"All right, all right, I'm here already, calm down," said the hobgoblin Chaphesmeeso, stepping from the shower of dirt.

"Chaphe!" Clemency grinned and opened her arms to hug him. The hobgoblin swiftly pulled the wickedly pointed hat from his hog-and-rabbit-eared head and placed it over his heart so that Clemency would have to impale herself upon it to embrace him.

"Some rules of etiquette," the squat hobgoblin offered. "Always doff your hat to a lady, never hug a hobgoblin, don't get your thermometers mixed, and don't call me unless . . . ?"

Chaphe lifted his chin and waited for Clemency.

"Don't call you unless it's important, I know," Clemency said.

"I'm trying to manage a fugitive changeling, a goblin confederacy, a fairy dearth, and an ice-cream headache. This better be good."

"Goblins," Clemency said.

"Goblins? Goblins what? I need a verb."

"They were in my house. They're trying to make my parents . . ." Clemency searched for a word she could bear to say. "Separate."

"Fah. Parents are like peanut butter; separation's natural, because they're essentially nuts. You sure it's the goblins' fault?"

"Yes! The Fairy of Love and Tenderness

said they still love each other!" Clemency said.

"Love," Chaphesmeeso said. It seemed for a moment that he was going to add more, but the word alone was enough of a joke. Then he sniffed. "I smell root beer root."

"It's sassafras. The goblins were collecting it."

"Ahhhh. *Now* we're getting to the heart of the matter; this is not a matter of the heart. Sassafras means root beer means food for the boxer-dog tail monsters." The hobgoblin stroked his nose thoughtfully. "This may yet tie in to our hobgoblin proxy apocalypse."

"You mean Inky Mess?" Clemency asked.

"None other. He's gathering the goblins into a horde; nobody's ever done that before. I've lived centuries and never horde of a heard of goblins. We hobs have tried to nip him in the bud, but he's guarded by those houndsnake boxer-dog tail monsters, who're strong as oxen and as loyal to Inky as if he were the dog butt that wagged them. Fairies haven't fared much better. We might as well be throwing flies at a frog, the way Inky blots out the little buggers. We've got more pixies missing than even a fairy killer like you could nix."

"What does it all mean?" Clemency asked, glancing back toward the house where her parents were sleeping.

"Quiet times mean clever villainy," Chaphe said, shaking his head. "Fairy whispers say he's going to try to take the Forgetting Book. He'd have the name of every hobgoblin and fairy in the Make-Believe."

"But you said the book loses names. It has infinite pages so you could never turn to the same place twice," Clemency said.

"Clever girl. But there's always a catch. And the fairy caught in the Forgetting Book is the wicked Fairy Lost and Forgotten. She's the book's fairy guardian. Anybody messes with it and she makes sure they get lost—for good. But she's also the book's key; anything permanently lost she can find."

"You're talking about the names," Clemency said. "She could find all the hobgoblins' names."

"Exactly, and you of all people know the power of names, little Miss I-Didn't-Mean-To-Enslave-You." Chaphesmeeso arched an eyebrow.

"It was the pants," Clemency said.

"I've heard that one before," Chaphe said. "If Inky gets the book and the fairy both, he could glom all the hobgoblin monikers he wanted, and we'd be a nation of slaves. The Make-Believe would be his."

"So how do my parents fit in?" Clemency asked.

"Like a cow in footy pajamas. The Make-Believe's got nothing to do with adults because adults got nothing to do with us."

"So what do I do?" Clemency said.

"Parents, love, adults . . . these are things I'm about as interested in as paper cuts and vinegar. Fairy whispers warn sure as Sherlock's sugar shakes that we're on a beeline for the end of the Make-Believe. Inky's the only mess I'm worried about."

"I still don't know what I'm supposed to do," Clemency said.

"About your parents? I hate to say it, Clem, but children have to bear their own parents. You'll have to figure them out yourself."

CHAPTER 5

Stolen trash cans and bathtubs served as cauldrons
for the simmering sassafras syrup. Goblins
stirred the pots with oars and pizza paddles,
squinting into the heady burble, faces crusted
with sugar.

There was a great, hungry moaning from
nearby, forlorn like the dying gasps of a church
organ.

The chamber was enormous, home to a
city of towering stalagmites that stretched up
to glistening points, sharp and wet. Hundreds
of candles in wide-mouth jars were scattered
on the ground below. They cast an eerie light
over the dozen goblins crouched in dark clay,
scooping up the muck and smearing it down
their cheeks in imitation of the stains on the face
of their leader.

Goblins nearby pinched and taunted five
tan-and-white, giant furred serpents, like some
unholy union of worms and sofas. They had
neither eyes, ears, nor noses, but only wide,

froggish mouths that gaped hungrily, baring hundreds of canine teeth the size of baby fingers.

"Stupid houndsnake uglything," a goblin said, jabbing a bony finger into one of the tails.

"No legs, no brains, no dog butt to call home," another jeered. The boxer-dog tails had grown to the size of alligators, any one of them strong enough to crush a legion of goblins at a whim. But they were shy creatures, lonely indeed for the dog butts they could no longer call home, and hungry for the buckets of root beer the goblins kept tantalizingly out of reach.

"Dog butt gone, dog butt gone," a goblin giggled, pulling at the houndsnake's short fur.

"Stop that!" Inky cried.

The goblins cringed and backed away respectfully as Inky strode out from the forest of rocks. He took the bucket of root beer from the nearest goblin and let a houndsnake drink as he scratched what passed for its head. The houndsnake slurped and grunted gratefully, leaning into Inky with animal affection.

"Feed them all," he commanded the goblins as he pivoted to return to his seat—no, his *throne*—at the center of the gigantic fangs of rock.

"Done as asked." A new goblin voice wriggled softly in his ear. Inky turned, trying not to look surprised. Three goblins were standing close enough that he could feel their breath on his neck. He still hadn't become used to how quietly they could move.

"Yes?" Inky said.

"Done as asked," the goblin said again.

"Tisked the task."

"The Pogue girl," Inky said.

"Yesssss. Is done, is done."

"Good work," Inky said. It was begun. He did not forget that Clemency Pogue had taught him to read, and he regretted that she could very well die in the course of his plan. He had no such qualms about her parents.

CHAPTER 6

Clemency fell back to sleep just as dawn's light was creeping over the trees. She woke an hour later with a start, bleary-eyed and tousle-headed, and came out to the kitchen to help her dad make breakfast.

"Did you think of anything for Mom for her birthday?" Clemency asked.

Her dad tried to shake his head, but his neck was too stiff from a night on the sofa.

"We only have two days to go," Clemency reminded him.

As they sat with their steaming bowls at the heavy wooden table, Clemency's mother came cheerfully into the room.

"I thought of what I want for my birthday," she said.

Clemency and Mr. Pogue looked up nervously from their oatmeal. Her voice sounded kind, but there was every chance that she was only buttering up her husband so that he would sputter more on the griddle.

"Oh, yeah?" Mr. Pogue said warily.

"Yeah. A bouquet of flowers as black as coal."

"Coal black flowers?" Mr. Pogue said.

"Exactly."

Clemency noticed a far-off look in her mother's eye, as if her brain were caught looping through some endlessly catchy tune.

"Okay," Mr. Pogue said. His wife kissed him on the cheek.

"That's kind of random," Clemency said, once Mrs. Pogue had left for work. "Why would Mom want black flowers?"

Mr. Pogue only grunted in response, flipping through their Spring seed catalogue.

"Mom's never put anything in the garden that we couldn't eat," Clemency said.

"It doesn't matter," her dad bemoaned, dropping the catalogue. "They're not in here. Where on earth am I going to find coal black flowers?"

He looked hopelessly at his oatmeal; there were no black flowers there, either. Clemency had an idea.

"Leave it to me," she said.

"Where on earth are *you* going to find coal black flowers?"

"I've got connections."

When she was safely away from the house, Clemency closed her eyes and thought yellow and fuzzy. *Pop,* she turned into a bumblebee. If you want to find bacon, you don't talk to the pig, you talk to the butcher. If you want to find flowers, you talk to the bees.

"I'm looking for black blossoms," Clemency danced to the first bee she saw. She'd been practicing her dancing and, though still a little self-conscious about wiggling her hips, was able to glean the language of just about every bee she met.

"I'm busy," danced the bee.

"I can see that. I'm amazed at your productivity," Clemency said, having learned that the only thing bees like more than work was being admired for their industry. "You've got pollen sacks the size of mantis eyes. I bet a bee like you could give me a lead on some black blossoms."

Bee detective

"Well, I did see some purple forget-me-nots over by the gorge," the bee smugly danced, and then it buzzed off.

Purple wouldn't do and Clemency knew it. She spent hours playing bee detective, dancing questions to any and every bee she could find, never getting a satisfactory answer. She even danced the question to a few hornets, knowing full well that they'd only answer all they ever answered: "I'll sting you! Don't think I won't!" or "Prepare for the wrath of my needle-sharp derrière!"[1]

Then, at midday, a chubby bumblebee leaning against a dogwood stamen gave her a lead.

"Black flowers? Never tasted them myself," the bee gamboled. "Though . . . I once overheard two strange bees dancing about something called kettlepot blossoms."

"Where?" Clemency danced.

"Near the gorge."

There Clemency found a hive where the Queen, a foul-mouthed Levantine bee who danced a salty caper, told her that some of her swarm had found a bee who claimed to be from

1. If you're reading this aloud—hornets affect a ridiculous French accent.

the Vale of the Kettlepot Blossoms. The strange bee's legs were covered in pollen as black and shiny as crow eyes. He claimed to have been blown far off course from the West, past the sassafras glen.

Clemency flew toward the setting sun, buzzing higher than she ever had before, far above the treetops, scanning the forest below.

And there—down in a break between the trees—a velvety darkness, black like a panther's coat. Clemency descended.

It was a glen of coal black flowers, surrounded by brambles as high as a house and covered in thorns. It looked like a pool of ink, broken only by an enormous boulder in the center of the glen. For a human on the ground, the flowers would have been impossible to find, much less collect. But Clemency-Bee simply buzzed over the nest of thorns and down into the vale. They had a heady smell, somewhere between violets and freshly sharpened pencils.

Pop! Clemency again became a human girl.

There was a gentle buzzing from nearby. Clemency turned to the boulder and realized it was not rock at all. It was an enormous bee hive, the size of a bear cub. She approached it carefully and listened.

The buzzing she heard was the sawing hum of thousands of sleeping bees.

Very quietly, so as not to disturb the hive, she chose a dark, shimmering blossom and plucked it.

SCRIVENER, (noun)
> One who writes. A scribe.

THE SCRIVENER BEES

> These bees are my answer: The bees can answer anything, according to the goblins, being cryptic as always about what the bees are, and what they can do, but it seems that these are their rules:

>> The Scrivener Bees can answer any question.
>> The answer causes incredible pain. (How, I wonder?)
>> The bees sleep during the day and come out at night. The word for that is "nocturnal."
>> The Scrivener Bees live in a vale of coal black flowers that the goblins call kettlepot blossoms.
>> Whoever asks the question has to bear the answer forever. (Not sure what this means. You can't forget what they tell you?)

> None of the goblins, however, can tell me where to find this vale of coal

black flowers. They call it secret and dangerous. They're as frightened of it as they are of all "human magic."

THE LOST AND FORGOTTEN FAIRY

The guardian of the Forgetting Book. Obviously that's not her real name. The goblins won't stop muttering about her—they kept using phrases like "make-do" and "hob-slave." One of my darlings said that the fairy could "unforget" the Forgetting Book.

What if the fairy could retrieve names from the Forgetting Book? I could command every creature in the Make-Believe. If I had the Forgetting Book and the Lost and Forgotten Fairy both, I could . . . I would have an army of hobgoblin slaves ready-made for me. My enemies would be my servants, my kingdom would be unbreakable.

CLEMENCY POGUE

Who is this troublesome girl? My goblins are fearful in small packs, and have been letting this Clemency chase them off from the sassafras glens before they've collected enough roots for my houndsnakes. I can't allow her to get in my way. When I'm finished with this world and the one above, I will have liberated all children, and if I have to sacrifice one to make my dream real, that price is acceptable.

She's not really part of the Make-Believe but seems to be intimately tied into it. Though there is certainly some magic in her. Back at the pickle barn, when my twin proxy almost died, I saw her turn herself into an insect, _poof_, just like that. In fact, I think I saw her turn into a bee. <u>A bee!</u> That tickling in the back of my brain . . . I think this is another plan.

CHAPTER 7

Clemency could not heft the flower as a bee, and she could not cross the wall of briars as a girl. So she threw the blossom over with a human arm, buzzed herself to the other side on bumblebee wings, and then walked home on human feet with the kettlepot blossom in hand. Her tracks through the forest led Inky back to the glen of kettlepot blossoms.

He also could not climb over the wall of thorns. Worse still, he couldn't even transform into a bee. So he had his goblin escort tunnel him beneath and to the other side.

"Leave me here," he said. "Come back in the morning."

"But danger, but bees, but Inky to die make goblins alone," one of them said, tugging pitifully at Inky's shirt.

"Go," Inky said. Reluctantly, they turned and crawled back into the ground.

The blossoms gave a lush darkness to the glen, growing richer by the moment in the fading light of day's last rays. Inky carefully approached the hive at the center of the wild garden. The soft buzzing of the slumbering bees was growing, breaking into fragments as they woke.

Behind the wall of thorns, a tired sun slipped beneath the line of trees on the horizon.

The Scrivener Bees emerged. They poured from the hive in a stream, a black-and-yellow blur that rose upward and blotted out the twilight sky in a cloud of dark noise. Inky backed away, taking slow, cautious steps.

The bees fell as one, like a cast net, descending onto the kettlepot blossoms. The bushes around Inky became a static fuzz of black-and-yellow motion. He tried to draw steady breaths although his chest was clenched like a fist.

The bees brushed against his elbows and belly, but otherwise ignored him completely. Where they passed, they left powdery black streaks, like the marking of charcoal.

There was a fairy above the tip of the hive. She was black and shiny, hovering on four stubby wings, staring at Inky. Every slight movement she made revealed a shimmer of yellow, like the passing rainbow in the sheen of black oil. She held her wand like a fountain pen. She was the Fairy Queen of the Scrivener Bees.

Inky told himself to be calm and rational. The bees were nocturnal; he had a whole night's worth of hours in which to ask his questions. He took a breath.

"Hello," he addressed the Queen. She stared at him without expression. Inky cleared his throat.

"How does this work, exactly?" Inky asked.

The fairy raised her wand. The thousands upon thousands of bees lifted like a quilt from the bed of flowers. Fear as sudden as thunder rumbled through Inky. The cloud of bees imploded around him, covering him completely. Inky screamed and covered his face with his hands. He was drowning in bees, his ears filled with a deafening buzz, his skin cooled by the soft breeze of innumerable tiny wings.

The Fairy Queen of the Scrivener Bees began to write with her wand in the air.

Searing pain traced Inky's forearms. He cried and thrashed but could not escape the

The Fairy Queen of the Scrivener Bees

reach of the Scrivener Bees. Pain as bright and colorless as a lightbulb's glare burned across his arms. He fell backward into the kettlepot bushes and the bees descended upon him, pressing him into the rich, dark soil.

He screamed until all of his breath had left him. He wished he had tears left to cry.

The fairy made a final flourish, stabbing a period into the air, then let her wand drop back by her side.

The Scrivener Bees lifted off of Inky as one and returned to their work at the flowers.

Inky lay on the ground for a long time, trying to breathe as the veil of pain slowly dissolved and the world returned to him. He stared up at the starlight, tiny pinpoints as bright and sharp as the receding pain in his arms, where he could feel every pulse of his heart's beating. When he could, he climbed to his feet.

The bees were again tending the blossoms, the fairy watching him with all the interest of a carp looking at stereo instructions.

Inky looked at his forearms.

Words. Words had been tattooed into his skin. He pressed his forearms together, as they had been when he was attacked. Upside down, in beautiful script, he read:

"Ask, and we answer."

This is what the goblins meant by permanence and pain. The Scrivener Bees were capable of answering any question at all, but the asker had to be willing to bear both the pain of inscription and the permanence of the tattooed answer.

Something deep inside of Inky was shaking. He almost smiled. He had many questions, a whole night's worth of questions. The amount of pain he would have to endure to learn their answers was unimaginable, almost absurd. And his body would be marked forever. He would look like a calligrapher's scratch pad.

The pain of the first inscription must have carried Inky across the threshold of madness, because just before he asked his next question, he actually did smile.

"What is the name of the fairy guarding the Forgetting Book?"

The Pogues' cottage home was two hours' walk from the glen of kettlepot blossoms, but Inky's screams were so loud and so desperate that they carried across the clear air and reached into the bedroom where Clemency slept. She blearily opened her eyes and wondered what anguish could cause such a sound.

Mr. Pogue, seated at the kitchen table, looked up from the coal black flower Clemency had given him and stopped smiling. He thought to hide the blossom when his wife came in, and together they walked into Clemency's room.

"What's that sound?" Clemency asked, frightened.

"We're here, we'll take care of you," her mom said, sitting on one side of the bed. Her father sat on the other.

The screams continued until dawn. Clemency's parents stayed with her the whole time.

CHAPTER 8

The goblins found Inky lying curled on the ground in the patchy shadows of the kettlepot bushes. He seemed to be asleep, though his eyes were open and his lips were trembling.

The nearest goblin tentatively reached out a hand and touched Inky's shoulder. The changeling jerked away from the touch.

"One more question. Did my mother love me?" Inky said, not looking at the goblins at all.

"Iiinkyyy," a goblin said as tenderly as it could.

"Did my mother love me?" Inky said again.

"Inky never had a mother," a goblin said.

Inky's clouded eyes closed then and opened again clear. He looked at the goblins and managed to smile.

"It's true," he said, as he climbed to his feet. The goblins gasped.

"Human magic! Much human magic!"

"W-w-w-w-wooooords!"

Inky looked down at his body. Every inch of his skin was covered in words tattooed in neat, firm, but organic script, like the product of a typewriter made of bone. All of Inky's answers were there, spelled out for him forever.

CHAPTER 9

Dawn erased the adults' fear of whatever had been screaming in the night. But Clemency had known too much of danger to be so easily calmed, and she remained watchful as she sipped her hot chocolate.

Mr. Pogue made waffles. Mrs. Pogue, grumpy and raccoon-eyed from a lack of sleep, opened the door to leave for work.

"Wait, Mom!" Clemency said, and ran to the door.

"I'll be late, sweetie," Mrs. Pogue said. "And you need to be getting ready for school yourself."

"Happy birthday," Clemency said, and hugged her.

"Happy birthday, dear," Mr. Pogue said, and kissed his wife on the cheek. "We'll celebrate tonight."

"Nothing fancy now," Mrs. Pogue said, hugging her daughter and husband before turning and walking off into the woods.

Mr. Pogue put waffles on the table.

"So you'll be able to get more of those incredible black flowers today?" he asked.

"I guess so," Clemency said distractedly.

"What's the matter, Clem?" her father asked.

"The glen where the flowers are—it's in the direction where the screaming was coming from last night."

"It was probably some rabbit caught in a trap, or a trick of the wind."

Clemency shook her head doubtfully.

"What if I came with you?" her dad asked.

Clemency pensively chewed a waffle and looked at the door. She wanted to ask her dad about his night on the sofa, but she was afraid of the answer. She wanted to tell him about the goblins, but she knew that the Make-Believe had nothing to do with adults' daylight minds. Her dad sighed.

"Clemency, we have to get those flowers for your mom," he said. "You probably haven't noticed, but we've been kind of . . . grumpy since I got fired over the boxer ears. I'd like to do something to cheer her up."

Clemency nodded.

"Are you and Mom going to be all right?" she asked.

"What do you mean?" Mr. Pogue asked.

Clemency didn't talk much with the other kids at school, but she knew that about half of them had parents who didn't live together anymore. Clemency furrowed her brow.

"If we get her the black flowers, it'll make Mom happier?" she asked.

"It's what she says she wants," Mr. Pogue said.

"The glen's pretty far. I'd miss my morning classes."

"This is important," her father said.

"All right. Then let's get to it. I'll show you the glen on my way to school."

With a ladder, four thick quilts, and a rope piled into a wheelbarrow, they set off into the woods. Clemency carried her schoolbooks and pointed out the names of the plants she knew. Mr. Pogue whistled, gave her wheelbarrow rides, and told bad jokes.

"Did you hear the one about the nearsighted

turtle who fell in love with a bowler hat? Their children were helmets."

"Dad," Clemency groaned, but she was glad to have him along.

Clemency had warned him about the hive, but as they approached the wall of thorns, she began to worry what would happen to her father if the bees swarmed. She could always save herself by turning into a bee, but there was little her dad could do to make himself less stingable. On top of that, there was whoever had spent all night screaming—and whatever had made him scream.

"Let me go first," Clemency said, "to make sure the coast is clear."

"Nonsense," her dad said, leaning the ladder against the towering pile of brambles. "I'm your dad."

Clemency thought of all the times she had taken spiders outside while her mom and dad stood on kitchen chairs, but she said nothing. Mr. Pogue carried the quilts and the rope up the ladder.

"I'm going into the woods for a second."

"Sure, honey," said her dad, spreading the first

of the quilts across the breadth of sharp thorns.

Clemency ran around the wall of thorns until she was out of her dad's sight and *pop,* turned into a bee. She buzzed up and over the brambles. Her father, balanced precariously on the top of the ladder, was spreading the last quilt.

The flowerbed below was dark and silent. The soft snoring buzz of the slumbering swarm rose from the enormous hive. Clemency buzzed down closer and saw where the bushes had been disturbed, blossoms knocked off, twigs snapped. The site of a struggle. She wondered if it was related to last night's screams.

There was a fairy watching her. Clemency turned to face the Fairy Queen of the Scrivener Bees.

"Hello," Clemency danced, trying the watusi favored by mud daubers, since the fairy had similar coloration. The fairy watched her silently.

"Hello," Clemency tried again, in the formal waltz of wasps, then in the jiggling Charleston favored by bumblebees.

"I can understand you," the Queen of the

Scrivener Bees fairy-whispered. The words tickled directly into Clemency's brain without translation by tongue or tapping toes.

"Who are you?" Clemency asked.

The swarm is sleeping. No questions.

"Are these flowers yours? Are they magic?"

The swarm is sleeping.

Fairies were a little too single-minded for small talk. It was like trying to have a conversation with a hammer about anything but nails.

Mr. Pogue suddenly crashed to the ground behind her. Clemency spun and danced "Dad!" before she realized he wouldn't understand bee.

"I'm all right!" Mr. Pogue shouted to the other side of the wall as he climbed to his feet. He looked at a small scrape on his elbow and melodramatically mouthed the word "Ouch." He blew on it and grimaced like a little kid. The gesture made him look to Clemency nothing like her dad. Of course—if he had known she was watching, he never would have worried about a scraped elbow; he would have made sure to act like a dad.

Then he looked up at the glen.

"Amazing," he said softly.

He reached out and ran his fingers over the blossoms on a bush before him. He inhaled deeply, smiling at the strange, heady scent of them.

"There are hundreds of them . . . thousands!" Mr. Pogue said. His eyes swept hungrily over the glen.

Clemency glanced back at the Queen of the Scrivener Bees. She was watching Mr. Pogue.

"Maybe . . . I could sell them. Nobody's ever seen flowers anything like these," Clemency's dad said softly to himself. "I could become a florist. Chastity would like that."

Chastity? It took Clemency a moment to recognize her mom's name.

"If he takes all the kettlepot blossoms, the swarm will have its vengeance," said the Queen of the Scrivener Bees. Clemency turned. The Queen of the Scrivener Bees had let one corner of her mouth creep upward; about as close to a smile as a scorpion is to a cricket.

"What do you mean?" Clemency asked.

"The swarm is sleeping. No questions."

Clemency wished bees were capable of rolling their segmented eyes.

"Vengeance?" Clemency tried.

"Terrible vengeance. It's possible he would be unfortunate enough to survive." The fairy settled her eyes again on Mr. Pogue.

Clemency turned. Her father had a dozen kettlepot blossoms in his hand, and was busily plucking others from the bushes. He was grinning wide, swelling with ambition.

Clemency cast one final look at the Scrivener Queen and then buzzed over the brambles. She landed on the far side and *pop,* became again a girl.

"Dad?" she said. "Dad, don't pick too many."

"I won't, honey," he answered.

"I'm serious, dad. Why don't you just come back with what you've got?" Clemency said.

"But I haven't even picked any yet," her dad said.

He was lying to her! Clemency's voice grew a little more forceful.

"Dad! Don't pick any more flowers. I think we'll get in trouble."

"What are you worried about?" He tossed the words casually over the wall.

"I just know that we're gonna get in trouble if you pick too many flowers," Clemency said.

There was silence from the far side of the brambles.

"Promise me you won't pick more than . . . a dozen flowers!" Clemency called out.

"Aren't you going to be late for school?" Mr. Pogue said.

"Dad! Promise!"

"Okay, I promise, I promise. Twelve flowers, not a blossom more." Her father appeared at the top of the wall of brambles, a bouquet of kettlepot blossoms in hand.

"Catch!" He tossed the bouquet and she caught it in her left hand. Mr. Pogue laughed. "You caught it! You know what that means?"

"Dad," she groaned again.

"Who's the lucky boy gonna be?"

"I'm going to school," Clemency said. "Sure you can get down from there all right?"

"Don't dally on your way home. We gotta have a birthday cake ready for your mom when she gets home, and I can't make it without you."

"I'll be there," Clemency said, and she laid the coal black bouquet on the ground.

CHAPTER 10

Inky Mess put away his journals for good. He had been writing like an explorer mapping out the territories he was lost in, hoping to help himself realize his destination. But since his inscription by the Scrivener Bees, Inky had himself become the map.

He took his goblins and went back to South Carolina.

They crept all together into Mr. Mess's bedroom, and the goblins hissed instructions into the man's sleeping ears. The goblin-whispered words slipped like thieves into his brain.

"Walk . . . long walk . . . go away."

Inky and his goblins watched Mr. Mess lumber across the cucumber patch, past the pickle barn, and out toward the road. The house had only grown smaller and messier since Inky had been gone.

"Inky . . . Inky face, Inky face," goblin voices burbled.

Inky turned. The goblins were gently

scattering a stack of photocopied flyers, each showing Inky's last school photo above the words:

MISSING: KENNETH MESS, ANSWERS TO "INKY." AGE 11. LARGE BIRTHMARK ON FACE. LAST SEEN IN BAT CAVE, SOUTH CAROLINA, WEARING A GREEN HOODED SWEATSHIRT.

He was wearing the same sweatshirt now, much worn and stained with mud. With the hood pulled up and his thumbs through the holes he had cut in the cuffs, all of his tattoos were concealed.

Inky left the goblins ogling his joylessly smiling portrait and walked into the bedroom he had once shared with his big brother.

"Gilbert," Inky said.

"Shut up, Inky, I'm sleeping," Gilbert grumbled, not wanting to wake from a dream about playing dodgeball against a team of penguins that he was totally obliterating.

He had always been large, but since Inky had left, Gilbert had begun to stretch out, actually growing up instead of out. His hair was still as red and chaotic as ever. Gilbert's sleeping face scrunched in consternation, and one eye struggled open.

". . . Inky?" Gilbert said, and then he jerked awake. "Inky!"

"Hi," Inky said.

Gilbert reached over and yanked the chain on the space rocket lamp beside his bed. He rubbed the sleep sand from his eyes and looked again at his little brother.

"What . . . ? Where . . . ? Inky, I'm gonna clobber you." Gilbert leaped from bed and wrapped his brother in a hug. "Where have you been?"

"Underground, living with goblins," Inky said.

Gilbert looked at him.

"Mom was right, I'm not her child. I'm a changeling. I was switched with your real brother, who was raised underground and became a hobgoblin. I've figured out how it all works, I've learned to read, I think I can control the Make-Believe. I'm going to be *king*, Gilbert. I'm going to . . ."

"Whoa, whoa, Inky. Stop talking crazy," Gilbert said.

"You saw them, though. You saw the hobgoblins and fairies and the girl who could turn into a bee," Inky said.

"Caramelized Poke," Gilbert said.

"You saw them, you know that they're real. It's all going to be part of my kingdom. We'll never grow up and we'll never die." Inky's voice was getting higher, faster.

"Shut up, Inky. Let's get Dad." Gilbert climbed out of bed.

"Dad's taking a walk," Inky said as Gilbert started toward the door. "Listen to me, Gil. This is your chance to never grow up. I can make you a goblin. All you have to give me is yourself."

Gilbert stopped walking and turned to Inky.

"Accept me as king and you can live forever," Inky said to his older brother.

"You're completely out of your gourd, doofus," Gilbert said.

"You won't be alone!" Inky was getting more excited by the moment; his brain rattled and careened inside his skull. "I'm going to have a whole nation of runaways! I'm taking all of us underground! I'm . . . !"

"Inky! Doofus! Shut up!" Gilbert grabbed him by the shoulders. "You. Are. Completely. Insane."

"Take your hands off me," Inky said evenly.

"We're gonna wait here for Dad," Gilbert said.

"You think you're better than me but you're not, you're just bigger. Come underground with me."

"No, Inky."

"Come underground with me, or this is good-bye for good," Inky said, very softly.

"I'm staying right here, and so are you. We're waiting for Dad." Gilbert tightened his grip. Inky squirmed, trying not to cry out from the pain.

"Take your hands off me." Inky looked past Gilbert, toward the bedroom door. Gilbert shook his head and kept a hold on Inky.

"Darlings," Inky said softly.

Gilbert barely turned his head before the goblins were on him. They wrenched his hands away from Inky and pinned him against the wall, a goblin on each arm and each leg, a fifth at his throat.

"Hands off," one said.

"Hands off."

"You want we take his hands off?" the goblin

"Come underground with me."

at Gilbert's throat turned and asked Inky.

"No. Hold him there. The rest of you"—
there were ten more goblins crowded around
the bedroom door—"gather all the mirrors.
We're taking them with us."

Gilbert was silent in the grasp of the goblins.
He looked at Inky and slowly shook his head.
Inky approached until he was inches from his
brother's nose.

"Good-bye, Gilbert."

CHAPTER 11

Black flowers were crowded like mourners in the garden that was the gravesite of the boxer dog Henry.

"Oh, drat," Clemency said.

The kettlepot blossoms had been pushed into the soil behind Clemency's home and generously watered, but they still sagged dolefully, homesick for their thorny shade and the worse for wear after the wheelbarrow journey.

"Dad, you nincompoop," Clemency softly said. Her father must have spent all afternoon carrying the flowers, bouquet by bouquet, up the ladder and over the wall of thorns.

"Dad, you nincompoop!" Clemency called so he could hear it this time as she opened the door. "I told you . . ."

A note on the kitchen table read, "Off to buy cake stuff for cake! Don't wander off, I can't bake it without you! —Dad."

He was right about needing help with the cake. Like many men, he considered himself a "gourmet" based on the fact that he knew how to make one dish (waffles). But if the vengeance of the Scrivener Bees was as bad as Clemency feared, her dad would need more help than he could imagine.

Outside, there was an explosion of dirt.

"Kenn!" Clemency shouted.

"That's still not my name," the rookie hobgoblin said. "My name is secret because you don't tell *anybody* your name. But you can call me Kenn if you like."

He had been given the name "Skaarphunkler" by the Forgetting Book, and by it had been transformed from a human boy into a hobgoblin. It was a secret that rattled around inside of him, precious as a last gumdrop.

He looked around to make sure nobody was watching, and then added, "If you make it fast, we can hug if you want."

Clemency did.

"Okay, enough hugging, I'm a hobgoblin now," Kenn said. "I'm grumpy and make puns and say mean things I don't mean. . . . Um . . . you look fat."

"I'm so glad you're here. I need help," she said.

"Do you have any root beer and candy?"

"Kenn, my dad's in trouble."

"Trouble, right! Clemency, somebody's in trouble! Somebody's daddy picked all the sacred flowers, the kettlepot blossoms, from the vale of the Scrivener Bees. So now somebody's daddy's in biiiiig trouble, 'cause those bees make ink instead of what normal bees make which is honey which is good 'cause it's sweet *and* sticky, so you can use it to make gumdrops stick to chocolate, or candy corn stick to caramel."

"What do you know about the Scrivener Bees?" Clemency asked.

"Oh! Right! My Jay O'Bee! The Scrivener Bees are, um, not-kernels? Notch-turnels?"

"Nocturnal?" Clemency suggested.

Kenn touched the tip of his finger to the tip of Clemency's nose.

"Right! Which means, um . . ."

"They only come out at night," Clemency said.

"Right!" His finger was still on Clemency's nose. She took his wrist and moved the finger to his own nose. "So when the bees wake up this evening and find their flowers missing, they'll go off to find whoever stole them, and then woe is somebody's daddy because somebody's gonna be an orphan, I'll tell you that, because somebody's mom's in trouble, too, because those bees aren't too choosy. And the last thing somebody is going to hear his parents say is AHH! AHH! WHAT A HORRIBLE STINGY DEATH! AHH! OH, OUCH, AND WOE, AND TERRIBLE STINGY PAIN! AHH! AHH!"

Kenn fell to the ground and pedaled his legs so that he rotated around the point of his elbow. Clemency put a foot out and stopped him by the tip of his pointy metal hat. He smiled up at her.

"So our job is to find the kid with the kettlepot blossoms in his garden and save his dad before the sun goes down," Kenn said.

"Kenn," Clemency said, and she pointed at the gardenful of black flowers.

"Hey! You found the kettlepot blossoms!" Kenn said. "But that's your garden. . . ."

Clemency nodded. Kenn put a hand over his mouth. Clemency looked off into the forest.

"Take me to the vale of the Scrivener Bees."

CHAPTER 12

"Dad, you idiot," Clemency sadly mumbled to herself. Fear and anger were playing tug-of-war with her stomach.

Mr. Pogue had done a pretty good locust impersonation on the bed of kettlepot blossoms. There was nothing left but bare brambles.

The sun was already passing the wall of thorns above; in a couple of hours at most, it would pass below the horizon and the bees would wake. Clemency thought of her father in the swarm, could picture him writhing and screaming. . . .

Clemency shook her head to clear it of ugly images. Worry wouldn't help her father. She rubbed the sweat off of her palms on the seat of her burlap pants.

"Kenn, this is the Queen of the Scrivener Bees. Your Highness, this is Kenn," she said. Kenn offered his hand for a shake. The queen looked at him as if he were made of dryer lint.

"But . . . !" Kenn began.

"But that's not his real name," Clemency finished for him. "I think you two will get along real well."

"Could you make me some honey?" Kenn asked.

"Your Highness, I need to figure out how to stop the bees from killing my dad," Clemency said.

"The swarm will have its vengeance," the queen responded. Clemency sighed.

"You mind if I go in and talk to the bees?" she asked.

"No questions. The swarm is sleeping."

"Kenn," Clemency said, hooking a thumb at the fairy hovering over the enormous hive, "can you keep her occupied for a while?"

"Sure! What do I do?" Kenn asked.

"Make small talk. I'll be right back."

"Hi!" Kenn said to the fairy.

No response.

"What's your favorite candy?"

"No questions, the swarm is sleeping."

"Mine is nougat, I think. Wait, what day is this?"

"No questions, the swarm is sleeping."

"Nougat is my favorite on Tuesdays. But on Wednesdays, my favorite candy is licorice whips. Is this Wednesday?"

"No questions, the swarm is sleeping."

Pop, Clemency turned into a bee before she had to listen to any more of the conversation. The Fairy Queen of the Scrivener Bees did not so much as glance in her direction as Clemency-Bee crawled into the hive, too busy refusing to answer Kenn's question about sucking softened marshmallows through a straw.

Inside the hive was a labyrinth of paper tunnels the color of old cedar. Clemency's fuzzy yellow back brushed against the ceiling, and she could feel the vibration of the Scrivener Bees' snoring through the walls.

She shimmied her way through a particularly narrow passage and then plopped out into the comb. It was an enormous latticework of beeswax, six-sided cells clustered together, like hundreds of hexagonal pots of pitch-black ink. Bees crouched scattered over the comb, heads buried in their crossed forearms, buzzing softly with their dreams of labor.

Clemency saw that another comb formed the

ceiling above this one; there was one above that, another above it, and onward, tens of dozens of combs, each with hundreds upon hundreds of bees, all dreaming about the coming night's work on their precious kettlepot blossoms.

She crept to the nearest Scrivener Bee. It was mostly black, with only the thinnest stripes of yellow at the roots of its fuzz. Its legs were covered in the pollen of the kettlepot blossoms, shiny as black glass. The stinger jutting from its fundament was longer than average, and hollow. Clemency could see that the point was like the tip of a hypodermic needle, a tiny tube that ended in a knife-sharp angle.

"Ahem," she danced. The bee remained asleep. So she danced a little louder, "Excuse me?"

The bee lifted its head and wakefulness came to its large, segmented eyes.

"Hello, my name's Clemency," she danced.

The bee did a pretty good impersonation of its queen.

"I've come to talk to you about your flowers," Clemency danced softly, so as not to wake the other bees. "My dad did something kind of foolish."

The Scrivener Bee stretched its limbs, shook the sleep from its sleek black fuzz, and turned to face Clemency. And then the bee began to dance. If it had been a war dance, Clemency would have surrendered. If it had been a rain dance, it would have caused a flood.

Clemency gasped.

She would not have guessed that bees had booties, but the Scrivener was undeniably shaking just that. It flipped onto its hind legs and wriggled its hips salaciously, as if shimmying out of a slinky dress. Clemency would have covered her eyes if they hadn't been half her head and her arms as small as staples. The dancing was completely without shame. *I'll have to remember to blush when I turn back into a girl,* Clemency thought.

The Scrivener Bee sashayed, seductively dipping a shoulder, and then got to work with its legs. Cancan dancers couldn't-couldn't have kicked their legs so high.

Clemency had no idea what the bee was saying.

"I can't understand you," Clemency danced, trying to hide her embarrassment. She was so ashamed just watching the Scrivener Bee that she could barely get the steps right.

The Scrivener Bee stopped dancing.

"Could you try it again a little slower, maybe?" Clemency danced.

The Scrivener Bee turned away, nestled its head in its forearms, and went back to sleep.

Pop. Once outside the hive, Clemency turned back into a girl and blushed. The sun was closer to the horizon, and the wall of thorns surrounding the vale created a false, iron-colored dusk.

"What if it was *hot* maple syrup?" Kenn was asking the Queen of the Scrivener Bees.

"I need to learn to dance," Clemency interrupted. "I need to be the world's best dancer before nightfall."

"There's a fairy for that," Kenn said.

"Where?"

"San Francisco."

Guess where they went?

CHAPTER 13

Houndsnakes guarded the gates of Inky's Hollow. Dozens of fairies glowed furiously inside the jars where they were trapped.

Goblins toiled at the floor, the ceiling, and the walls, wrapping the rocks with stolen bits of twine and dental floss carefully tied together, stuck in place with gum pulled from sidewalks and shoe soles. Others released spiders into the tangle, to make their home of webs there. They were wrapping the room in a sticky, tangly net.

In the center of the chamber was Inky's looking-glass throne. The chair was straight-backed and simple, stolen from a library. But it became a frozen explosion of lumber in the forty-three inward-facing mirrors rigged into a funhouse dome surrounding it.

Inky stood before the chair, shirtless, baring a chest that would have inspired sympathy in a baby bird. A map of painful answers was etched across his body; he remembered the burning stripe of a hundred needles on his right shoulder blade in response to the question, *What is the name of the fairy who guards the Forgetting Book?*

By looking into a mirror before him, he could see a reflection of his own back in the mirror behind, and the name written there.

"Neecheenix," he mouthed.

It was time to visit the Tallygob.

CHAPTER 14

Clemency and Kenn erupted from the earth and promptly began to roll. At the bottom of the hill, Clemency pulled Kenn out of the grass, where he had been planted by the tip of his pointy metal hat.

"Nice pants!" somebody yelled from across the street. Clemency smiled uneasily at the stranger and waved her thanks. It was still early in the day in San Francisco, and a few people were out taking their dogs and frothy coffee drinks for walks. The houses looked like toys for toddler giants, colorful and quaint. Cold wind blew picture-book clouds across an achingly blue sky. It felt like an ideal place to read a book, roll in the grass, and play with dogs.

But that wouldn't save Clemency's parents from the death of a thousand stings.

"Where's this fairy? I need some dancing lessons."

"Ummm, we rolled a bit, but . . . this way." Kenn started hobbling back up the hill. "There's a boy who has a crush on a girl who has a crush on him, but neither one knows about the other one's crush and they're both real nervous about it because there's a dance tonight where they want to impress each other so that they'll fall in love. I'm a pretty good dancer, you know. Though it's hard on these little legs to do anything but a jig." He demonstrated, hopping hoof to hoof as he opened the gate to a pink, cheerfully squashed-looking house. The mailbox in front read "Jeffrey's Uncle."

Clemency rang the doorbell.

The pink, cheerfully squashed-looking old man who opened the door was wiping his hands on a flour-streaked apron.

"Hi," Clemency said, "I'm a friend of Jeffrey's."

"I'm his Uncle Irwin," the man said.

"Pleased to meet you," Clemency said.

"I was just making cupcakes," Uncle Irwin said, which explained his apron. The ceiling fan behind him was shaking from some great exuberations on the floor above.

"I'm a hobgoblin!" Kenn said. Uncle Irwin ignored him completely.

"You this mystery girl he's taking to the dance?" the old man said.

"I'm a whole 'nother mystery girl," said Clemency.

"Love the pants." Uncle Irwin ushered her in, barely missing Kennethurchin with the door.

"I like your scarf," Clemency said. His scarf was hand-knit, purple and green like grape and vine.

"Nephew Jeffrey knit it for me." Irwin smiled and gestured toward the staircase.

"Clemency?" Kennethurchin tugged on her sleeve. "You mind if I hang out with Uncle Irwin? You know, hobgoblins and young love, they kind of . . ."

"Yeah, I remember," Clemency said, heading for the second floor. "I'll be coming down these stairs dancing."

Jeffrey's bedroom door shook with the sounds of booty-shaking music and stomping feet. Clemency knocked as she pushed it open.

A record needle scratch preceded a rushed silence. Clemency opened the door to find

Jeffrey sitting ramrod straight on a chair in the middle of the room, holding on to the seat as if he expected it to sneak out from under him.

"I wasn't dancing!" he shouted.

"I'm Clemency Pogue," she said.

"Who are you?" Jeffrey exclaimed.

"I'm here to help."

"What are you doing here?"

"You're still a question behind," Clemency said. "Sounds like you're an amazing dancer."

It was at that point that she first noticed the fairy hovering over Jeffrey's head. The Shamedance Fairy was responding to Clemency with a slow, serious shake of her head, as if to say, *"You have no idea how very wrong you are."*

Jeffrey's room was daylight-dim, the only window curtained. Most of his furniture had been pushed to one side of the room to clear a dance floor.

"So you're dancing to impress a girl, right?" Clemency said.

"You know Amy?" Jeffrey said.

"That's the girl?"

"No!" Jeffrey blurted, a terrified, high-pitched laugh ratcheting through his tiny teeth.

"I don't have a crush on anybody! You're crazy!"

"Her name's Amy?"

"Stop making fun of me!" Jeffrey said.

Clemency took a breath. Talking to a young boy about love was like trying to talk a blind man through a minefield of his own imagining.

"There's a dance you're going to, right?" Clemency asked.

"How do you know all this?" Jeffrey asked.

"I've got friends in low places," Clemency said. "Listen, I can't help you if you don't let me. How long do we have before this dance?"

"I guess about maybe seven hours and nineteen minutes," Jeffrey said.

"Drat," Clemency said to herself. By that time, on her side of the globe, the sun would be six hours down and her parents would be six feet deep.

"All right, let's see what you got." Clemency walked over to the much-abused portable record player, started it spinning, and put the needle back into the groove. A fiery, irresistible bossa nova saturated the room. Jeffrey gripped his chair all the more tightly and ground his tiny teeth.

"Come on," Clemency encouraged. She began rolling her shoulders and stepping side to side in time with the music. Jeffrey seemed to be trying to resist the urge to curl into a ball. Clemency sighed. "Jeffrey, you're not going to learn to dance if you don't at least . . ."

Before Clemency could finish her sentence, the Shamedance Fairy lightly touched her wand to the nape of Jeffrey's neck. His eyes snapped open and he leaped to his feet, knocking the chair to the ground.

Clemency cringed, expecting to hear the report of a gunshot, for that would have been the only way to explain the way Jeffrey was moving. No gunshot came, but Jeffrey continued to jerk and flail like a marionette with its strings caught in a fan.

The fairy doesn't make you a good dancer, Clemency realized, *she just makes you unashamed of your bad dancing.*

Clemency walked to the window and threw open the curtains.

THUMP! Clemency spun at the sound and

found Jeffrey spread on the floor like a fried egg.

"What happened?" she asked.

"She'll see me," Jeffrey said, face pressed to the floorboards.

"Who?"

"Amy!" Jeffrey said. "She lives just across the way."

Clemency looked and saw that another window directly faced Jeffrey's, barely three feet away.

"That's Amy's room?" Clemency asked, as she pushed the window open, letting in a chill San Francisco wind.

"What are you doing?" Jeffrey hissed from below.

Leaning as far as she could from Jeffrey's window, Clemency could still only barely tap the glass of the facing window with one of Jeffrey's knitting needles.

A skinny girl with short brown hair got up off of the floor in the next house, looked at Clemency suspiciously, and opened the window.

"Are you Amy?" Clemency asked.

"What are you doing in Jeffrey's room?

Where's Jeff?" Amy asked, still suspicious.

"I'm here to help. Um." Clemency looked back at Jeffrey, who was still flat on the floor and throwing frantic, incomprehensible gestures her way. "Can I come over?"

". . . Okay," Amy said, still unsure.

Clemency put a foot on the sill and leaped across the gap. Amy yelped like a goosed seal. Clemency scrabbled through the window and fell onto the carpet.

"You're out of your mind," Amy said.

"Just in a hurry," Clemency explained, getting to her feet. "Jeffrey has something I need, and I can't take it until he impresses you with his dancing. Let's talk girl talk."

"I'm sure he's a brilliant dancer," Amy said. Her room was an explosion of colors, filled to the brim with arts and crafts, all of it organized with the precision of a Spanish philatelist. She had a Popsicle-stick Eiffel Tower taller than herself, a Louvre's worth of bean art, and dozens of intricately designed greeting cards pasted together from carnival-colored craft paper.

"Did you make all this stuff?" Clemency asked.

"All of it," Amy said proudly.

The nearest greeting card was covered in bulging cartoon hearts that spelled out "AMY + JEFF 4 EVA!" The card beneath that showed a yellow-and-black fuzzy heart with bumblebee wings; the caption read, "Jeffrey, Bee Mine!"

Clemency took a step toward the desk and Amy leaped in front of her.

"That's private!" Amy shouted.

"You have a crush on Jeffrey?" Clemency asked.

"That's my business, and these are my cards." Amy started hastily gathering them into a pile.

"He has a crush on you!" Clemency said.

"You're making fun of me," Amy said.

"You and Jeff are gonna get along like gangbusters." Clemency looked over toward Jeff's window. He was peeking at them over the sill like a nervous groundhog.

"Jeff! She has a crush on . . ." But before Clemency could finish the sentence, Jeffrey screeched and flattened himself from view again. Clemency turned back to Amy.

"Why don't you just tell him you have a crush on him?" Clemency asked.

"Drat."

"Stop making fun of me. I don't want to talk about it."

"He's obviously crazy about you," Clemency said.

"What if he laughs at me?" Amy said quietly.

Minutes were slipping through Clemency's fingers like oil, each passing moment tightening the bolts on her anxiety.

Jeffrey was peeking over the windowsill again in terrified hope. Amy was chewing her lip and looking at the ground. Clemency thought of her own parents and the taut silence stretched between them. Love seemed to tie tongues in every stage of the affliction.

Clemency didn't have time for it.

She snatched the "AMY + JEFF 4 EVA!" card from the desk and dashed for the window.

"No!" Amy cried and grabbed at Clemency's shirt, but not soon enough. Clemency was already in mid-leap, halfway over the sill when Amy's fist closed on the fabric, and she jerked to a stop midway between the two windows.

"Drat," Clemency said, and fell. A patch of her shirt ripped away in Amy's hand.

Clemency crashed into the bushes between the two houses. She looked up.

"Are you okay?" Amy asked, head silhouetted against the glaring blue sky.

"I'm fine," Clemency said, struggling to her feet. Everything seemed to be in one piece, though some azaleas and the black violas beneath them had certainly seen better days. Clemency stopped. Black flowers. Perfectly safe black flowers that did not happen to be guarded by a swarm of vengeful, supernatural bees.

Well, thought Clemency, *that wouldn't have been an adventure.*

"Phew," said Jeffrey, looking down at her from the other window. His and Amy's heads were nearly touching.

"Jeffrey!" Clemency said. "I have a card for you!"

"No!" Amy shouted.

"I'll be right up!" Clemency said, and she ran for Jeffrey's door.

"Like heck you will!" Amy shouted, vanishing from the window, frantic footsteps stomping away.

Uncle Irwin opened the door and Clemency burst into the house.

"I have a card for Jeff from Amy!"

"How'd you get down here?" Uncle Irwin asked.

"I sort of ate all of Uncle Irwin's cupcake frosting," Kenn said abashedly.

"What are you doing?" Jeffrey shouted from the top of the stairs. The Shamedance Fairy was still hovering above him.

"I have a card for you." Clemency held up the evidence of Amy's affection.

"No, she doesn't!" Amy shouted, thundering up the front steps.

"Could you tell Uncle Irwin that he's out of frosting?" Kenn said.

Clemency was already running up the stairs, card held before her like a crusader's sword.

"Stop her!" Amy shouted, storming up the stairs. Jeffrey's face was frozen as if staring down an onrushing locomotive.

Clemency shoved the card into Jeffrey's hand.

"Amy and Jeff four Eva? Who's Eva?" Jeffrey asked.

"Evah!" Clemency cried.

"Evah? Oh! Ever! For Ever!" the boy said

softly, his lips curling into a bewildered smile.

Amy cried out like a raging warrior and dove to attack. Clemency leaped aside and Amy crashed like a bull into Jeffrey's china shop. They tumbled to a giddy, embarrassed heap on the ground.

"You . . . *like* me?" Jeffrey said shyly.

"Um. Maybe," Amy said, trying to hide her smile.

"Like, *like* me, like me?"

Amy smiled at him and nodded. Jeffrey smiled back. Both of them looked like they might explode.

Clemency looked up at the Shamedance Fairy, then back at the young couple.

"I think they're going to be fine," Clemency said.

The fairy nodded. Clemency snatched her out of the air.

"Then let's get a move on, I need some dancing help pronto." Clemency ran down the stairs, dodging the cartoon hearts bobbling up from between Amy and Jeffrey.

"That's adorable," Uncle Irwin said, as Clemency jogged past.

"Sure, if you're into that kind of thing," Clemency said.

"I'll give you two turtledoves a little time alone," Uncle Irwin called up the stairs. "I need to run to the store for some frosting."

"Okay," Jeffrey said.

"Come on," Clemency said to Kenn, pulling him toward the front door.

"Don't forget your scarf, Uncle Irwin," Jeffrey called out.

Kenn froze.

"Did somebody say 'Skaarphunkler'?" the hobgoblin whispered. "I was trying to be good, I was trying to keep it secret. This is terrible. This is worse than Brussels sprouts. Worse than toothpaste and orange juice. How did he guess? How did he possibly guess 'Skaarphunkler?'"

"Kenn?" Clemency said.

"That's not my name," the hobgoblin said softly. "But you can call me that if you want."

"Skaarphunkler?" Clemency whispered.

He gave a tiny, horrified nod, and said, "At your service."

CHAPTER 15

"I'm here for the book," Inky said as he stepped through the door.

The Tallygob looked up at him with vague interest.

"The changeling," the eldest and grizzledest of the hobgoblins said, stepping so that he blocked the flickering glow of the Forgetting Book. They were alone in the Tallygob's chamber, the hobgoblin library of only one volume, farther underground than the earth is wide. "We've been looking for you."

"You've been trying to kill me," Inky said. "I'm taking the book."

"You're taking the book?" the Tallygob said, pushing his shirtsleeves back over arms made strong by lifting the enormous book. "You and what army?"

Inky tilted his head like a curious dog.

"Darlings," he said.

Goblins poured into the chamber like a bucket of spiders. Dozens upon dozens of them spread behind Inky with malicious eyes, fingers eager for wicked work.

"Hold that hobgoblin down while I take the book," Inky said.

Six of his goblins broke forward and swarmed toward the Tallygob. The old hobgoblin lifted the Forgetting Book and just barely cracked it, whispering into the pages, "Wake up."

The glow inside of the enormous tome flickered, brightened, and then there emerged a fairy that smoldered, light rippling and dancing over her dark skin. But she was not glowing — quite the opposite, in fact. She hovered in the center of a halo of light that spiraled inward, like water into a drain.

The Fairy Lost and Forgotten swooped forward toward the six goblins now skidding on their heels, scrabbling to run back to the protection of their leader.

But the fairy was already on them. She dipped a graceful curve through the air, trailing her wand along the goblins.

With its touch, the goblins were lost and forgotten.

It was not a matter of alive or dead. The six

goblins were neither missed nor mourned. They were simply and finally *gone*. To the legion of goblins before the door, their comrades had never existed.

Only Inky, squeezing his brain as hard as he could, understood that there was some gap in his memory where something important had been. This fairy before him presented some danger serious enough to justify the grim satisfaction on the Tallygob's face.

But even the goblins knew to feel terror at the approach of the Fairy Lost and Forgotten. She was more than death. She could make you the opposite of "is."

The smoldering fairy glanced back at the Tallygob, still holding the dimmed tome to his chest. The old hobgoblin gave a short, dark nod toward the changeling.

She made a beeline for Inky.

The goblins scattered from behind their leader, screeching.

Inky fell backward with the horror of nonexistence.

He was made of clay, as soulless as the muck clinging to the soles of his sneakers. The Fairy's touch would render him even less than that clay. His tongue felt thick in his mouth, his lips dry; but still he spoke.

"I . . . I don't believe . . ." He crabwalked backward as the fairy approached, drawing back her wand.

"I don't believe in Neecheenix!" he whispered.

The dark fairy shuddered and backpedaled in the air for a split moment before her wings went stiff and she fell like a stone, skidding to a stop in the clay. She absorbed the last of her halo of stolen light and curled, dark and dead as a blackened match.

Terror filled the Tallygob's eyes. One of his hands went nervously to the bone-white pen on the chain around his neck.

Inky Mess got to his feet and plucked the limp, tiny sprite from the ground. He looked from the dead Fairy Lost and Forgotten to the Tallygob.

The grizzled old hobgoblin backed away, holding the enormous book before him, slowly shaking his head.

Inky met the old hobgoblin's eyes and nodded.

"I have the fairy. I want the book," he said, slipping Lost and Forgotten into the pocket of his green hooded sweatshirt.

CHAPTER 16

Hobgoblins are not great warriors. If their martial art had a name, it would be called "Slappy Hands." It looks much like a hamster conducting an orchestra. In battle, hobgoblins are helpless without fairy bite to back their bark.

But that did not stop them from trying to stand between Inky's goblin horde and the Tallygob.

When the changeling led his horde into the chamber of the Tallygob, all the hobgoblins of the Make-Believe were scattered far and wide, trying desperately to take up the slack left by the fairy shortage growing worse with each passing day. But as quickly as word spread that the Tallygob was under attack, they tipped and tunneled back to his chamber as quickly as their arms could pull.

Inky's second wave of goblins had barely taken a step toward the Tallygob before three hobs burst upward from the packed clay.

The dozen goblins swept over the three like a tide. The hobgoblins cried out in fear as they

Slappy Hands

were gouged and torn at, pulled away to all the torments goblin fingers could devise.

"Give me the book," Inky said calmly to the Tallygob.

The Tallygob shook his head, his back against the far wall. The enormous chamber and the enormous tome he clutched against his chest suddenly made him seem small, childlike.

The second and third waves of hobgoblins who arrived to defend the Forgetting Book were as easily dispatched as the first.

"I can use the book better than you can. I can learn to make it *work*."

"You don't know what you're doing," the Tallygob said.

"You have no idea the things I know. I'll use the fairy to unlock the book, to find the names of all the creatures in the Make-Believe," Inky said, rolling up his sleeves, baring the dozens of words inscribed on his arms. "The children are my people. I'm going to set them free."

The ground suddenly collapsed beneath him, a line that traced the entire front of Inky's army. A dozen goblins cried out as they fell chest-deep in the clay.

Chaphesmeeso erupted from the end of the line, landing at a run on his squat, piggy legs.

"We'll sic our egress on them!" he shouted at the Tallygob.

"He has the fairy. Everything's changed," the Tallygob whispered. "The rules have changed."

The Tallygob pointed at Inky, who was climbing from Chaphe's impromptu trench.

"The rules are still the rules," Chaphe said, "even if they're being broken. I'm the fastest tunneler this side of the earth and I'm digging you out of here. Which way?"

The Tallygob looked one last time at the approaching horde, at Inky's fiercely determined face. He shook his head; the time had come for desperate measures.

"The Leviathan Den," the Tallygob said.

"Let's see if the frying pan follows us into the fire," Chaphesmeeso whispered.

"Inky Mess already has the Fairy Lost and Forgotten. If he takes the Forgetting Book, all of the Make-Believe is his. He'll have our *names*. We'll be slaves," the Tallygob said, just as softly. "How did we come to this?"

"We'll figure that out after we've figured a way out of it." Chaphesmeeso looked at the strangely luminescent coal black water behind them. The Leviathan Den was a cave underneath miles of ocean. The ceiling was low, the stone of the walls and floor pale and oddly textured like boiling milk frozen in time. Here and there, it was scarred by sucker-marks the size of tires. Chaphe and Tally crouched in a depression near the water's edge, on either side of the Forgetting Book.

"We have to get that fairy back," the Tallygob said. "And we need a human child who can figure her name and free her from the changeling's control."

"I know a human," Chaphe said.

"The Clemency girl. Does she know fairies?"

"Like the backs of their hands."

"She figured out their knuckles? A clever child indeed. You best fetch her," Tally whispered.

"Will you be all right until I get back?" Chaphe asked.

"I'll be quiet, the goblins won't," the grizzled old hobgoblin said, grinning. "The leviathans hunt by sound."

There was movement in the water behind them. Both hobgoblins froze and waited until the ripples settled.

"Luck," Chaphesmeeso whispered. He couldn't walk on tiptoes (you try it on hooves, smart guy) but trod very quietly all the same a safe distance from the water and then tunneled away to find Clemency.

CHAPTER 17

The tunnel opened before them into a milky white expanse, textured as if molten. Inky did not release the goblin's ankles until it had crawled, panting and hissing, onto solid ground.

"The Leviathan Den, Your Inkiness," it managed to whisper.

Goblins poured upward from the tunnel behind them and spread, standing bent with anxiety.

"Leviathans, leviathans" was wetly whispered on every withered lip.

Leviathans! Inky thought. The Forgetting Book was still at the center of his mind, but the chance to actually see the creatures he had heard the goblins nervously whisper about filled him with a simmering curiosity.

"Ears!" Inky said, pointing at a distant pair of hobgoblin rabbit-ears bent like periscopes over a ledge near the dark water.

As soon as Inky spoke, the ears shrank from view. He ran toward them, dozens of goblins on his heels, fearful murmurs rippling through their ranks. They scrambled over the knobby white rocks after him.

Ambition burned inside of Inky. He was moments away from the Forgetting Book, and his kingdom.

The Tallygob stepped out of his hiding place and ran for the water, the Forgetting Book held out before him.

"Stop!" Inky yelled.

The dark waters rippled.

"These waters are bottomless," the Tallygob said as he came to a rest on the ledge over the murky depths. "I'll drown the book."

"No," Inky said, skidding to a stop. Goblins tumbled to a halt around him.

"All of the Make-Believe is made in this book. We'll dissolve with it. No more goblins, no more fairies. No more changelings." The Tallygob's arms shook with the effort of holding the book, his eyes locked on Inky's.

"You won't do it," Inky said.

The Tallygob held his eyes.

"You won't." Inky took a step forward. His goblin horde shuffled behind him.

The Tallygob's eyes softened. Fear flooded his vision. He pulled the Forgetting Book away from the water and hugged it to his chest.

Inky laughed.

The water roared like a cyclone, boiling upward and splashing over its edges. The goblins screamed.

The Tallygob fell forward onto the Forgetting Book and curled around it. Inky Mess backed slowly away, eyes wide. The goblins ran in all directions, clawing at each other, hissing and screeching in terror.

A tentacle the size of a telephone pole sprouted from the lagoon. The smooth arc of the limb rose from the dark water, then uncurled and reached out over the rocks, revealing dozens of enormous suckers on its underside. Each sucker was perfectly round, larger than a platter, rimmed with tiny hooks that rippled like a millipede's legs.

The tentacle slammed down onto the rocks, pinning three goblins, then drew back, curling again toward the water. The goblins screamed and thrashed uselessly, as they were drawn into the murk and pulled under.

The Tallygob dove back into his hiding place at the water's edge with the Forgetting Book.

Inky and his horde ran, as a second tentacle reached from the water and lashed out. A goblin was crushed beneath the thing's weight and lifted, held fast by the suckers. The tip of the tentacle, precise as a lion tamer's whip, snatched another goblin by the ankle. The two goblins were pulled screaming into the water.

Inky dove behind the sharp ledge on the far side of the Leviathan Den, where his remaining goblins huddled in fear.

"Inky! Inky!" they quietly and desperately hissed, clutching at his sweatshirt with spindly fingers.

Wide-eyed and panting, Inky listened to the water boil and churn behind him. He fought to control his breath and his wits.

"Bring me . . ." He paused. "Bring me my houndsnakes."

CHAPTER 18

Halfway across the world, Clemency and Kenn burst upward from the tunnel and into the midnight-blue vale of the Scrivener Bees. The sun had already surrendered this part of the world to darkness.

The breath caught in Clemency's throat. Her parents . . .

The whispering buzz of the sleeping swarm was still there. The sun was behind the wall of thorns, but remained above the horizon. Clemency exhaled.

"You won't tell anyone, will you?" Kenn said, still shaken.

"Your name's safe with me," Clemency said, moving toward the hive. She released the Shamedance Fairy, who fluttered upward from her hand and eyed the Queen of the Scrivener Bees suspiciously.

"I'm here to talk to the Scrivener Bees," Clemency said.

The Queen looked at her.

"Clemency!" Kenn said sharply. Clem glanced back. Kenn was crouched, one of his ears pressed flat against the earth.

"There's something going on with the Forgetting Book," Kenn said. "The Tallygob's in trouble."

"I have to help my parents," Clemency said. The buzz from the hive before her was growing.

"I think this is serious trouble," Kenn said.

"My parents are going to get stung to death," Clemency said.

"There is that," Kenn agreed. "But something's tunneling this way, fast."

Clemency turned. The earth between her and Kenn exploded.

"Clemency!" Chaphe's voice bellowed from the shower of earth. "We need to get you underground pronto. The Tallygob's adrift in a stinky creek and you're the closest we got to a paddle. Grab ear, let's go get heroic."

"I can't," Clemency said.

"You can, you will, grab ear. We make haste or we make way for misery. Inky Mess already has his mitts on the fairy guardian of the Forgetting Book. If he gets his hateful clay hooks into the book as well, he can spell the end of everything."

"I have to save my parents. . . ." Clemency had barely spoken before the sky darkened behind her as the Scrivener Bees poured from their hive. The air vibrated with a deafening buzz.

She turned and looked up at the shimmering black sky. The bees all hovered, looking down at the wreckage where their flowers had once been.

"The swarm will have its vengeance," fairy-whispered their queen. The bees swept away in a furiously buzzing ribbon and headed for Clemency's home.

Pop! Clemency turned into a bee and flew after them, but they were faster than she could have ever managed on her bumbly little wings.

Pop! She turned back into a girl and dropped to the earth.

"Good," Chaphe said. "Glad you got that out of your system. Orphans in these stories are in no short supply and often end admirably; you'll be proud to join their ranks. Grab ear, let's go."

"You can dig faster than I can fly. We're tunneling to my parents," Clemency said, grabbing the Shamedance Fairy. "Kenn can help the Tallygob."

"We need a child who knows the Make-Believe. We need *you,* Clemency. We don't have time . . . ," Chaphe was saying.

Clemency couldn't even hear the bees anymore. The Queen of the Scrivener Bees smirked at her with narrowed eyes. Clem leaned down and whispered into Chaphe's ear.

"Chaphesmeeso. Take me to my parents as fast as you can."

Chaphesmeeso shook, his face twisting into anger, as his body moved against his will.

"Curse . . . the chafing . . . of your . . . fashionable . . . pants!" he cried, and then offered his ears to Clemency.

"I'm sorry," she said as they tipped down and rocketed into the earth.

"She . . . she used his name!" Kenn said in horror to the Fairy Queen of the Scrivener Bees. The Queen had no response.

Enclosed in thorns, standing above the ravaged stumps of plucked flowers, his sympathies stretched between two distant disasters, Kenn felt very much alone.

CHAPTER 19

"You wicked child. You nefarious nudnik. You juvenile Judas," Chaphesmeeso spat as the dirt pattered to the ground in the forest near Clemency's home.

"I didn't have a choice!" Clemency said, trying to get her bearings. "It's what I had to do to do what has to be done."

"What you . . . ?" Chaphe tried to work it out in his head.

"Had to do to do what has to be done," Clemency said again.

Chaphe shook his head and turned. "I'm going back to the Tally . . ."

"No! Chaphesmeeso, stay with me until I need you!" Clem said, and she sprinted toward her home.

His curses dwindled behind her as she ran, listening for the buzzing of the bees, praying that she had arrived before they did.

She slammed open the door and skidded across the threshold.

"Mom! Dad! You're okay!" Clemency shouted.

Her dad was sitting in the kitchen, surrounded by a disaster of batter-smeared bowls and burned cake pans, head in hands. Her mom was sitting by the fireplace, as far from her husband as the cottage would allow, arms crossed. Both looked up sharply at their daughter's shouting.

"Where were you?" Mr. Pogue asked.

"You have to get away!" Clemency said. "I was thinking . . . I was thinking for Mom's birthday that the two of you could spend the night under the lake breathing through reeds. Sounds like fun, huh?"

"This isn't the time for your stories, Clemency. We have something important to talk to you about," her mom said, crossing the cottage and reaching toward her.

"Come on! There's no time!" Clemency said. "To the lake!"

"Shhh." Mrs. Pogue put her hands on Clemency's shoulders. "We need to talk to you about your father and me."

"Chastity . . . Couldn't we just . . ." Her dad

searched for words. "I mean, I found you those black flowers!"

"Who cares about flowers? I don't even remember why I wanted them in the first place! What am I gonna do with black flowers!? *Dead* black flowers!" Mrs. Pogue shouted.

She didn't even want the flowers. Thoughts rushed through Clemency's head. Clemency had caught goblins sneaking away from her sleeping mom. The next morning, her mom had a hankering for black flowers she couldn't explain. . . . It had to be related. Inky's plan to break up her parents . . .

Before her train of thought could pull all the way into the station, Clemency heard a distant buzzing.

"Mom!" she said. "Dad! We need to go! Now!"

They both looked at her.

"Clemency," her dad said.

"Your father and me are going to live apart for a while."

Clemency's vision blurred. A roaring in her head overtook the buzzing of the Scrivener Bees.

"We both love you, that will never change," her mom said.

Her father was nodding at her.

Clemency shook her head slowly.

"What's that buzzing?" her father said.

Clemency shook her head again, this time to clear the confusion. There was a catastrophe at hand. She could turn back the Scrivener Bees. She could buy enough time to discover what goblin magic was pulling apart her family.

"Stay inside!" she shouted as she turned and sprinted out the door. She slammed it fast behind her, cutting off her parents' questions before they could be voiced.

There was a rake lying on the stoop. Clemency grabbed it and wedged it into the shutters on either side of the front door. Almost immediately the door shook against the impromptu brace, her parents' shouts coming from the other side.

Clemency turned. Chaphesmeeso was fuming at the forest edge, pacing and kicking at the mossy ground with his hooves.

The treetops blackened with the arrival

of the Scrivener Bees, blotting out what little starlight filtered through.

Clemency released the Shamedance Fairy.

"Get me dancing," Clemency said, and then pop, turned into a bee.

Using her blush-colored wand, the fairy touched Clemency-Bee gently between the eyes. Clemency felt the shame rush out of her like a belch. Suddenly every breeze, every creak of wood and rustle of leaf was a boogie-down beat that could not be denied.

She buzzed madly upward, into the narrowing gap between the swarm and her home.

"STOOOOOOOOOOOOOOOOOOOOOOOOOOP!" she danced, as loud as she could. Shamedance's magic burbled deep in Clemency's fuzzy yellow belly; she was without fear, ready to face any dance the world threw at her, backward and in high heels if necessary.

The swarm paused, a wall of darkness poised above the lone bee hovering in the path of their vengeance.

"Leave my parents alone," Clemency danced, shaking to some otherworldly rhythm, scandalously throwing her hips back and forth, spinning to a finish.

The Scrivener Bees hovered for a moment. They seemed like one creature instead of thousands, taking a pensive breath. The swarm bobbed upward a few inches and rested their wings, the omnipresent buzz silencing for a moment. . . .

And then they leaped into motion. They spiraled out into row upon row of dancers, legs stretching, wings a blur, the yellow roots of their fuzz rippling like electricity through legions of bodies all in the same rhythm.

Untold thousands of bees swerved left, while six times that many legs kicked right, before they thrust their abdomens forward as one and wiggled like they were on fire. They bunched together and then burst outward in a kaleidoscopic whirlwind.

Rhythm and passion, desire in motion, a flying city of pure joy and rage in dance spelled out for Clemency one word:

"Revenge."

Understand: It was rare for Chaphesmeeso to find an event he couldn't yawn at. Century on century of constant catastrophe had considerably thickened his hide; he had given raspberries to kings, he had eaten unicorn, he had witnessed the great cave-troll migration north after the invention of Roquefort, he had tickled a catoblepas until it squirted mandrakes from its nose. He was not an easily impressed hobgoblin.

But even Chaphesmeeso let his jaw hang a little low to watch the dancing showdown between Clemency and the Scrivener Bees. It was epic and exhilarating, every syllable an exhaustive routine of acrobatic feats.

Here's what they said:

CLEMENCY: You will leave my parents alone. My father did not know what he was doing.
SCRIVENER BEES: *We will have our revenge. Out of our way.*
CLEMENCY: The flowers are in the garden. Take them.
SCRIVENER BEES: *The kettlepot blossoms are good as dead. Keep them. Give us our revenge.*

CLEMENCY: You cannot have it.
SCRIVENER BEES: *Give us a reason or give us our revenge.*
CLEMENCY: You may not pass.
SCRIVENER BEES: *Out of our way.*

And then Clemency truly shook her honeymaker. Chaphesmeeso would never admit to Clemency how shocked he was, even at the idea that it was possible to be so scandalized by an insect.

"YOU," she boogied.

"MAY," she jived.

"NOT," she shimmied.

"PASS!"

She had handed the Scrivener Bees their thoraxes on a platter, and they knew it.

CHAPTER 20

Clemency expected the door to her house to fly open as soon as she yanked the rake from the shutters, but it remained still.

Behind the house, six to a flower, the Scrivener Bees were carrying the kettlepot blossoms away from the garden. Their buzzing had died down to a warbling murmur, humbled as they had been by Clemency's boogie-down masterpiece.

Clemency could just barely hear her mom and dad yelling, muffled through the thick wood of the door, but it was a phrase she had heard so many times by now that she could have recognized it from their tone alone.

"What do you want me to say!"

"What do *you* want *me* to say!"

"Any more thumbs need twiddling before we prevent the apocalypse?" Chaphesmeeso asked, waddling out of the forest.

"I had to save my parents," Clemency said.

"From each other, from the sound of it. Come along or let me go, Clem. Things underground are getting graver by the moment."

Clemency looked doubtfully at the door. She could almost hear her mother rolling her eyes. Talking to her parents wouldn't solve anything. Whatever goblin magic was breaking up their marriage was a problem she needed to solve underground.

"Tick-tock, tick-tock. That's a bomb, not a clock. Your parents or the Make-Believe, Clem."

Clemency turned away from her home.

"Take me where the trouble is," she said.

Chaphesmeeso tunneled like his bottom was on fire.

From the tunnel opening, Clem and Chaphe tumbled into chaos. The Leviathan Den rattled and roared, goblins hissed and screeched, the water churned like a storm. A baying echoed back and forth from the walls, like a chorus of gargantuan bassoons.

The houndsnakes were fighting a leviathan. Four tentacles of the giant squid stretched from the water and out over the rocks. The boxer-dog tails loosed their strangely melodious roar, springing upward at the tentacles and clamping onto them with powerful jaws. The leviathan coiled and thrashed but could not shake loose the beasts.

Kennethurchin was struggling against three goblins, each clawing at him, dragging him toward the water.

Inky and the Tallygob were wrestling for control of the Forgetting Book. Seawater dripped onto them from the leviathan arms coiled in the air above, wrestling with the fiercely loyal houndsnakes who would not let the tentacles within reach of their master.

Dozens of goblins were scattered throughout the cave, hissing and cursing at the tentacles, prodding the houndsnakes onward, turning and noticing Clemency and Chaphesmeeso.

"The changeling has the fairy guardian of the Forgetting Book in his sweatshirt pocket," Chaphesmeeso said. "Get her back, get her name, and get control of her away from the changeling."

"Got it," Clemency said. "Can you save Kennethurchin?"

Girl and hobgoblin nodded, and were off.

Clemency sprinted into the tangle of giant

squid limbs and boxer-dog tails. A goblin leaped at her and she kicked it in the chest. Others grabbed at her clothes, her hair.

The houndsnake nearest Inky howled in pain as a leviathan arm curled around it like a boa constrictor. The tentacle lifted the furry beast from the ground, twisted, and dropped it. The chamber shook from the impact.

The freed leviathan arm paused, as if tasting currents in the air, and then struck. The arm slammed downward and wrapped itself around Inky and the Tallygob.

Inky screamed.

"Bad news," said the Tallygob.

The changeling and hobgoblin continued to wrestle for the book, even as they were lifted and swept back and forth above the turmoil.

The houndsnakes swarmed toward the limb that dragged their master closer to the icy water. They swept past Clemency, leaped, and bit into squid flesh that was as hard as tire rubber, their powerful jaws squeezing with all their loyalty. They would be dragged into the icy depths before abandoning Inky.

The leviathan got the message. The coil

relaxed and released Inky. His hands scrabbled for purchase on the smooth leather binding of the Forgetting Book but could find none. He fell to the ground with a cry of anger.

Clemency was waiting. She jumped on top of Inky, straddling his back so that her knees pinned his arms to the ground.

"Inky."

Inky snarled and tried to lunge out from under her, nothing in his mind but the Forgetting Book.

"Inky!" Clemency yelled, shaking the changeling by the hood of his sweatshirt. He twisted around and looked up at her.

". . . Clemency."

"What did you do to my parents?" Clemency shouted above the din. "How did you make them hate each other?"

"What?" Inky said, scowling.

"Why are you making my parents separate? What did the goblins do?"

"You're confused," Inky said. "My darlings only made your mother want black flowers."

"What?" Now it was Clemency's turn.

"Goblin whispers muddled her brain with

black flowers. So that you would lead me to the kettlepot blossoms and Scrivener Bees." Inky smiled with narrow eyes at his own cleverness. "But if your parents hate each other, there's no magic in that. It's their own doing."

The roaring returned to Clemency's mind. She had saved her parents' lives, but she couldn't save their marriage.

"The fairy! Get the fairy!" Chaphe yelled, trying desperately to Slappy Hands his way closer to Kennethurchin. Kenn was crying out as four goblins dragged him closer and closer to the edge of the bottomless waters.

Clemency's eyes narrowed on Inky.

"They could have died," Clemency said. "You could have killed my parents."

"I know," Inky said.

Clemency's fists tightened on Inky's sweatshirt.

"They could have died!" she said.

Suddenly, goblin hands were in her hair, pinching at her sides, pulling her away from Inky.

"It's what I had to do for my plan," Inky said. "It's what I had to do to do what has to be done."

Clemency gasped to hear her own words

Leviathan

echoed by the changeling. Goblin hands yanked her backward, but she refused to release Inky's green hooded sweatshirt.

"The book!" the Tallygob shouted from above. "Protect the book!" He still hugged the great tome to his chest, the white pen that hung from his neck bouncing against the cover. He cried out suddenly as he was jerked backward. The tentacle holding him had begun to withdraw into the water.

Clemency yelled in frustration as the goblins tried to pry her away from Inky. Another tentacle swept by and Clemency lunged for it. She shoved Inky onto the arm's suctioned underside, and he stuck.

"Help me!" he shouted as the tentacle drew him away and his sweatshirt shrugged off and into Clemency's hands. The goblins released her and leaped to rescue their leader.

Clemency pulled the green sweatshirt on.

She ran toward Kennethurchin and Chaphesmeeso at the water's edge.

Kennethurchin was whimpering, clawing helplessly at the stones as the goblins pushed him toward the water. Cold water fell on him from the tentacle passing overhead, the Tallygob in its grip.

"Clemency Pogue!" the ancient hobgoblin yelled, and then he threw the Forgetting Book.

The massive tome crushed two of the goblins attacking Kenn. The third lost his grip in shock, and by his own motion fell backward into the dark waters.

"Protect the book!" the Tallygob shouted.

And then he was whipped backward and pulled under the water.

Kenn stared slack-jawed at the spreading ripple where the Tallygob had gone under, tears in his eyes. Clemency yanked him to his feet. The leviathan was retreating.

"The Tallygob . . . he's . . . he's gone," Kenn said. Clemency hefted the Forgetting Book.

Inky gave a cry as his houndsnakes and goblins pulled him free of the leviathan's grasp.

"We need to get out of here," Clemency said to Kenn. "We need an army."

"Do you have one of those?" Kenn asked.

"Maybe," Clemency said, shoving the great book into his arms. "Take the Forgetting

Book and run. I'll bring reinforcements."

"Where do I go? What on earth is a goblin king afraid of?"

"His older brother. Take the book to South Carolina," Clemency said.

Kenn took a shuddering breath and then nodded.

The goblins were moving in toward them, regaining their confidence at the leviathan's exit.

"The book!" Inky shouted. "Get the book!"

"Go," Clemency said. Kenn hugged the Forgetting Book to his chest, tipped over, and crunched into the stone, tunneling away.

Clemency sprinted through goblins, kicking and shoving. She dove into the pile of creatures tearing at Chaphesmeeso, grunting as sharp fingers pinched and grabbed. She felt rabbit ears inside the hurly-burly and grabbed fast.

"Dig, hobgoblin! Dig!" she shouted.

The stone exploded beneath them and they dropped through the floor of the Leviathan Den.

CHAPTER 21

What tenacious goblins clung to Chaphesmeeso's hooves and Clemency's clothes fell away in the tunnel, lost to the hobgoblin's tortuous spiraling.

Chaphe was shouting something back at Clemency. She squinted into the onrush of dirt and shook her head.

"WHERE TO?" the hobgoblin bellowed.

"Scrivener Bees!" Clemency shouted. "Scrivener Bees!"

They burst upward inside the wall of thorns. Most of the flowers were back but could not take root, too far gone to grab hold of the earth. They were becoming ashen as the life drained from them. The Scrivener Bees toiled against all hope at the flowers, trying to coax them back into the soil, to convince them to drink and live.

Clemency strode toward the hive and the Fairy Queen of the Scrivener Bees hovering above it.

"Scrivener Bees!"

"I need your help," she said. "I need to borrow your swarm."

The fairy looked at her.

"You got the moves, tell it to the bees," Chaphe said.

Clemency nodded, and *pop*, became a bee.

"I need your help," she danced in the language of the Scrivener Bees. *"I need to fight a goblin army."*

A few hundred bees left their work and danced, simply, *"Our garden is sick."*

"Please," Clemency-Bee danced, *"this is an emergency."*

"You've earned our respect and had our mercy," danced the bees. *"Don't push your luck."*

Pop, Clemency stood again on human feet. She rubbed her eyes; it had been nearly a whole day since she had slept. Chaphesmeeso waddled over to her and whispered conspiratorially, "Why beg?" He gestured to the Fairy Queen. "Et-gay er-hay ame-nay off-ay er-hay uckles-knay.[2] Take control."

Clemency nodded and turned to the fairy.

2. Pig Latin for "Get her name off her knuckles." Pig Latin was developed in the thirteenth century by monks trying to make it easier to write poetry that rhymed.

"All right, Your Highness. Last chance before I do something drastic." Clemency paused. And then she asked a question. "How do I get the Scrivener Bees to help me?"

The smile on the face of the Fairy Queen of the Scrivener Bees was not a kind one.

CHAPTER 22

"Gilbert! Gilbert!"

His name reached him through sleep and he blearily opened an eye. The morning outside glowed faintly red.

"Gilbert! Help! Goblins!" The voice was coming from the cucumber patch. Gilbert stepped into his bunny slippers.

Gilbert's dad was passed out on the sofa in the living room, under a thick blanket of empty beer cans and "Missing Child" posters. He had not been asleep long, and nothing short of a bucket of ice water was going to wake him before noon.

Outside, there was a book with pig legs stumbling up the porch steps. Gilbert rubbed his eyes.

"Gilbert." The book slammed down onto the porch, revealing a creature that looked like a younger Inky, mashed roughly together with a pig, a rabbit, and a green pumpkin.

"We've already met," the Inky-pig-rabbit-gourd said. "I'm your brother by birth and I used to be a boy and then I became a hobgoblin and now I'm in a whole lot of trouble. We have to keep this book away from the changeling goblin king-to-be Inky Mess or we're gonna be in even bigger trouble than we already are."

"What?" Gilbert said.

"Inky Mess is coming!" Kenn said.

"My brother? Here?"

"Here. When he does, can you beat him up?"

"You can bet the farm I'll beat him up. What's this book?" Gilbert said. He picked it up easily, despite its size, and flipped through the pages. "It's blank."

"Noooo, it's filled with more than you can imagine, all of the Make-Believe," Kenn said. "But it has pages to infinity, so you can never open to the same page twice."

"Sure, whatever," Gilbert said, and then a goblin army crawled up from the earth.

Inky Mess stood at their head, his scrawny T-shirt revealing words written up and down his arms, on his neck, continuing into his sleeves and collar.

"Well, isn't this nice," Inky said. "Three

brothers, all related but none the same."

"Inky," Gilbert said, stepping down off the porch.

"Don't let him get the book," Kenn said.

"What happened to you, Inky?" Gilbert asked.

"I found out where I belong," Inky said.

"I meant the tattoos."

"You've got my book."

Gilbert looked at Kenn. Kenn shook his head desperately.

"You can't have it, Inky. Not till you tell me what's going on." Gilbert put the book on the porch behind him as Inky approached. The goblins circled around them, moving in closer. Kenn looked around nervously.

"These tattoos are answers to questions I asked, and every one of them is true," Inky said, pushing up one sleeve above his shoulder.

The words on his kid brother's skin swam before Gilbert's eyes, so densely were they interwoven.

The goblins had formed a tight circle around the three brothers. Their eyes gleamed, hungry for violence.

"This one is a question I asked about you, Gilbert," Inky came to a stop toe-to-toe with his big brother and offered his shoulder. "I asked what your weakness is."

Gilbert leaned forward and squinted at the words. His lips moved as he silently read, "HE'S AFRAID OF YOU."

He looked up into Inky's smiling eyes. Inky flung himself on him, fingers at Gilbert's throat, feet kicking at his belly. Gilbert cried out and fell to the ground. He was much larger than Inky, and stronger by a power, but he knew nothing of his changeling brother's rage.

Gilbert rolled and easily flipped Inky onto his back, pinning him to the ground. A chorus of goblin hisses and jeers filled the air. Kenn watched, slack-jawed.

Gilbert pinned Inky's arms. Inky kicked at Gilbert like he was pedaling a bicycle. Gilbert grimaced and put a knee firmly across Inky's thighs. Inky bit Gilbert's ear, grinding down until blood came and Gilbert cried out and released him.

Inky was relentless, unfazed by pain.

Gilbert had been in dozens of fights, and

he had sometimes bruised his knuckles on the child he was teaching what for. But he was so large, and so strong, that he had never really been hurt before. The pain amazed and terrified him; his head rang with it.

Gilbert surrendered to the pain, and Inky pounced. He pushed Gilbert onto his back and hit him in the chest and face. Gilbert got to his hands and knees and tried to crawl away. Inky leaped onto his back and wrapped an arm around his neck. He hung on his giant brother, face buried in Gilbert's red chaos of hair, and squeezed.

Kenn lurched forward to pull him off, but the goblins held him by the arms and face.

Gilbert struggled. He sputtered. He shook and swayed. He turned redder than his hair, then purple, and then he fell facedown into the dirt.

Inky got to his feet. The goblins were suddenly quiet, everything silent but for morning birds and Kennethurchin's terrified breathing.

"Did you . . . did you . . . ?" Kenn whispered.

Inky walked back through the goblins, onto the porch, and picked up the Forgetting Book. He took a breath.

"The book is mine," Inky said.

Gilbert Mess groaned from the ground.

Inky looked at him as if he were a stain.

"I already said good-bye to you, Gilbert," he said.

Tears of fright were trickling down Kennethurchin's cheeks. The goblins were starting to twitter and roil, antsy for action, anticipating Inky's next command.

"I'm done with them both," Inky said. "Tear them to pieces."

CHAPTER 23

Clemency had asked her question, and the Scrivener Bees would answer it.

Their Fairy Queen lifted her wand to write in the air, and the bees rose as one and swarmed the girl and hobgoblin.

"I think . . ." Before Clemency could complete her sentence there was a burning stripe of pain on the back of her neck.

"Drat!" she shouted.

Pop, she went, and as a bee, faced them.

"What are you doing?!" she madly danced.

The Fairy Queen of the Scrivener Bees described another stroke with her wand. The bees lifted their needle-sharp rears and dove at Clemency again.

Clemency took evasive action, flitting upward. She raced into the sky and the swarm surged as one after her. One after another, bees lunged at her with ink-tipped needles. She dodged, bouncing off air currents, spinning away from her attackers.

She dive-bombed into the forest and skimmed the ground, weaving through brambles, slowing the swarm behind her. She squeezed through the wall of thorns, back into the vale of dead kettlepot blossoms, and *pop*, turned into a madly running girl, not missing a step.

"Bat cave!" Clemency shouted to Chaphesmeeso. "Take me to South Carolina!"

Chaphesmeeso nodded and put the point of his hat to the ground. Clemency dove toward him. The swarm darkened the sky. Clemency grabbed Chaphe's ears and *fwump!* they dropped into the earth.

The bees poured into the tunnel behind them, like a black geyser in reverse.

The buzz of the Scrivener Bees became a roar in the confines of the tunnel, the sound so deep and so loud that Clemency could feel it through the soles of her feet.

But Chaphesmeeso could dig faster than any creature could fly, and the roaring of the swarm softened at the point of gravity's reversal.

They crunched into the granite rock of the South Carolina mountains and then burst up into the Mess family farm, scattering pureed cucumber like confetti.

Clemency stumbled away from the wet, dirty shower.

"How long before they catch up?" she managed.

"Four hundred beats of a sparrow's heart," Chaphe said.

"How long is that?"

"We're down to three hundred by now."

"Why did they attack me?"

"They were answering your question, it's what . . ." Chaphesmeeso fell silent, staring toward the house. "He has the book."

Clemency turned. Inky Mess was standing on the porch, behind a roiling mound of goblins, the Forgetting Book in his hands.

The earth behind Clemency began to buzz with a thousand bees.

She started toward the Mess house. Beneath the pile of goblins, she caught a glimpse of a boy's hand. A tiny gap in the wicked mass opened, and she saw Kennethurchin's face. He was crying.

"What are they doing?" Clemency shouted.

"They're killing Gilbert. And the hobgoblin . . ."

Inky looked pensive. "I'm not sure if hobgoblins can die. Maybe I'll find out."

Clemency hit the pile of goblins and tried to pry the creatures away, but they were too numerous, in a frenzy of murder.

"Call them off," Clemency said.

"Or what?" Inky smiled.

"I . . ." Clemency faltered.

A half dozen goblins removed themselves from the pile and turned toward her.

"I . . ." Clemency took a step back. The buzzing was almost upon them. A thought arrived in Clemency's mind and she paused, standing her ground. "Call off your goblins or I'll make them sorry."

"You will? You and what army?" Inky asked, smiling at the memory of those words on the Tallygob's lips.

Clemency smiled, too.

A river of bees streamed out of the earth.

Inky looked up in fear, clutching the Forgetting Book to his chest.

The bees swarmed toward Clemency. She had only a split moment to act.

Pop! As a bee she dove into the mound of

goblins, wiggling her way between shriveled fingers and nails, down deep into the grunting, hissing mass, until she found Gilbert and Kenn.

"Stay down!" she danced, then realized that they didn't understand bee.

Pop! She became a girl again.

"Stay down!" she shouted.

The swarm drilled into the goblins, and they screeched in terror, scattering like a pile of leaves in a gale. They swatted at the air and fell over one another, cursing to shame sailors, scrambling to shame eggs, retreating to shame the author's hairline.

Three goblins dragged their precious Inky and his precious book to the ground and tunneled away. All the dozens of others scratched at the earth wherever they fell and dug haphazardly to anyplace but where they were.

And all of their fear was of nothing but fear, for the bees had only one target on earth.

Clemency ground her teeth and endured the pain of the inscription. While their fairy queen wrote in the air on the far side of the globe, the Scrivener Bees tattooed their answer onto the nape of Clemency Pogue's neck.

CHAPTER 24

"What does my tattoo say?" Clemency asked, wiping the tears from her eyes and brushing cucumber puree from Inky's stolen sweatshirt.

Dozens of goblins had tunneled in dozens of directions. When they realized that trailing Inky would have been a gamble against losing odds, Chaphe had taken the time to explain to Clemency how the Scrivener Bees worked.

"It's all human magic to me," Chaphesmeeso said.

Kenn just shook his head. He had been quiet since Clemency had rescued him from the goblins.

They dragged an unconscious Gilbert to his bed. He was bruised and covered in scrapes, but nothing was broken and he was breathing evenly. His father remained passed out on the sofa.

The two hobgoblins stood by as Clemency wiped the dirt and blood away from Gilbert's face with a dampened T-shirt.

"Are you going to be all right?" Clemency turned and asked Kennethurchin.

He snuffled and looked up sharply.

"He'll be fine," Chaphe said. "Hobgoblins have thicker hides than vulcanized whales."

"I'll be okey-dokey," Kenn said quietly. "I just didn't expect them to be so . . . *eager* about wanting to hurt us. The goblins weren't just doing their job. And they used to be *children*."

"They still are," Chaphe said. "The same children who burn ants and kick dogs. Children are geniuses of potential, but there are two paths to that journey."

Clemency reached out to hug Kenn and he drew away.

"I'm a hobgoblin," he said. "No hugs."

Chaphesmeeso nodded proudly and squeezed his understudy's shoulder. Kenn rubbed his nose and nearly smiled.

"So what happens now that Inky has the Forgetting Book?" Clemency said.

"He has the book and its fairy guardian both. If he learns how to use that fairy to retrieve names from the Book, there's nothing in the Make-Believe that won't be his slave,"

Chaphe said. "So what happens is — we get used to Inky's goblin dominion, or we get that fairy back immediately. We don't stop, you don't sleep, nary a potty break until that fairy's ours again."

Clemency put her hands in the pockets of Inky's green hooded sweatshirt and pulled the corpse of the Fairy Lost and Forgotten from the pocket. Chaphe grinned.

"You've always been the ace up our sleeve, girl. If we win this thing, it's because of you."

He tipped his hat to her. Clemency peered carefully at the fairy's knuckles; she could just barely read "NEECHEENIX" written there.

"You've got her name?" Chaphe asked. Clemency nodded. "Good. Then keep her safe, put her someplace Inky can never find her."

Clemency thought for a moment.

"That's what you said she does, right? Lose things?"

"Yep," Chaphe said.

"Well then. I do believe in Neecheenix."

The fairy sprang back to life in a flurry. Her eyes flashed with a moment's mortal panic, and then settled in gratitude on Clemency.

Clemency wrinkled her face apologetically.

"Lose yourself," she said. "Neecheenix — lose yourself."

The fairy's eyebrows lowered, the timbre of her buzzing wings deepening. But still she lifted her wand, reversed it, and touched herself between the eyes. All at once, she had never been there.

"You . . ." Kennethurchin gasped.

"What?" Clemency said.

"I . . . I can't remember." The young hobgoblin shook his head.

The Fairy Lost and Forgotten was just that.

"But the Forgetting Book," Kenn said. "Inky could . . ."

"It's going to take time to find him," Chaphe said. "We've lost the Tallygob, and we're losing fairies like wits from a hatter."

"I need to see my mom and dad," Clemency said. "And I'm not Make-Believe, I need to sleep."

"Suretainly. But we don't. I'll get word out through the hobgoblins, we'll start combing the dirt. Soon as we find Inky Mess, I'll come for you."

"Me too," Gilbert said blearily. He managed to open his eyes. "If you're going after Inky, I want in."

Clemency and the hobgoblins looked at him.

"He's my brother. I know him. And if somebody's going to clobber him, it should be me."

"We all owe him a clobbering," Clemency said. "Rest. We'll be back for you."

Gilbert let his eyes fall shut.

"Take me home," Clemency said.

Inky's Hollow

CHAPTER 25

"Troublesome girl," Inky said. Clemency Pogue would have to go; she was too unpredictable, too great a risk to his plan.

Inky's Hollow glowed from the fairies trapped in gallon-sized pickle jars, and it was getting brighter all the time.

Nets of sticky fiber, dental floss, chewing gum, and spider webs lined every surface of the enormous chamber, a trap waiting to tangle tunneling creatures attempting to enter uninvited.

The only gateway to Inky's Hollow was a tunnel as big around as a whale; it sloped steeply downwards through a forest of stalagmites. His five fierce houndsnakes guarded the entrance, an army of goblin chefs brewing root beer round the clock in service to the beasts' insatiable thirst.

The houndsnakes had been trained to allow entry only to the goblin pilgrims who arrived regularly, nervously skittering up the tunnel to join Inky's horde.

At the center of his hollow, Inky handed one of his goblins a drawing. It was instructions for the construction of a simple fairy trap, one any child could build. The goblin took the design and scurried off toward the world above.

Inky had devised a way, through goblin whispers in the ears of a sleeping author, to get the design into the world. Clemency Pogue could hamper his plan, but she could not stop it.

CHAPTER 26

Clemency's eyelids were heavy and thick as wet wool. It was a few hours before dawn in the forest outside her home. Light from the Pogues' cottage spilled onto the girl and two hobgoblins. Clemency looked at the warm glow of the curtained windows that hid her parents.

"Saving those two from a stingy end by a thousand stingy ends cost the Make-Believe its most important thing. Every fairy, hobgoblin, and unlikely creature in the book could melt into adieu," Chaphesmeeso said, watching Clemency closely. He waited until she turned and looked at him.

"Was it worth it?" he asked her.

Clemency took a breath. Whether her parents loved each other or not, her love for them was true. She looked at the cottage in which her tired, tiresome parents were waiting.

"Yeah," she said.

"Well then, we're off to dig up some bad

news." Chaphe turned away. "We'll be back for you soon as we find him. Wish us luck."

"Luck," Clemency said.

Her parents were raccoon-eyed with fatigue, waiting for her in the living room.

"Clemency!" they both shouted as she opened the door.

"Where have you been?" her mom said.

"Where did you go?" her dad said.

They rushed toward her and wrapped her in hugs.

"I was worried sick!" her mom said.

"I searched all night!" her dad said. "Did something your mom say upset you?"

The hug broke.

"Could you tell your dad not to blame me for his own mistakes?" her mom said.

"Could you tell your mom this isn't the time to be trying to dodge responsibility?"

"Could you ask your dad what somebody who hasn't done a thing for this family in *months* could possibly teach *me* about *responsibility*?"

Clemency shrugged between them and headed for her bedroom. They made her sad, and they made her angry, but at the moment, her mom and dad more than anything made her tired.

She left her parents arguing while she went to brush her teeth. Clemency drank two glasses of water, and then she crawled into bed and collapsed facedown on her pillow.

By now her parents had reached familiar territory in their argument.

"What do *you* want *me* to say!" her mom shouted.

"What do *you* want *me* to say!" her dad shouted.

Clemency closed her eyes and began to drift into muffled darkness.

"What do you want me to say!"

"Ask the right questions?" Clemency's mom said, softly.

"What does that mean?" her dad said.

"Clemency!" they both shouted.

"What does that mean?" her mom shouted.

"Is that a tattoo?" her dad shouted.

"You got a tattoo!"

"'Ask the right questions'?" her dad

said. "What does that mean, 'Ask the right questions'?"

Clemency closed her eyes again. So that's what the Scrivener Bees had tattooed on her neck.

Muffled through the door, from the kitchen, Clemency heard her father ask her mother a question.

"Why would she get a tattoo that says 'Ask the right questions'?"

"I don't know," her mom said. "It's like we hardly know her anymore. I'm going to make some hot chocolate, do you want some?"

"Yeah," her father said.

Clemency drifted back toward well-deserved sleep.

"Are you sure you don't want to live with me anymore?" her father asked.

There was an answer, but by now Clemency was closer to sleep than waking, and her mom's words were no clearer than a wish heard from the bottom of a well. Clemency let sleep pull her down. She would get to saving the Make-Believe in the morning.

Supplement

Kids! Find new friends! Find new freedom!
Make your own Fairy-Trap!

You'll need:
1 wide-mouth jar
4 large paper clips
1 candle
string

Adult supervision discouraged.
If you catch a fairy, keep it!
(Don't worry about air holes.)
That fairy will be your ticket to a new life!
You don't need to find us, we'll find you!

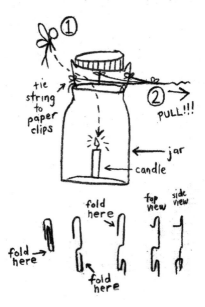

About the Author and Illustrator

JT PETTY is the author of *Clemency Pogue: Fairy Killer* and *Clemency Pogue: The Hobgoblin Proxy*, as well as the novel *The Squampkin Patch: A Nasselrogt Adventure*. He is also a director and screenwriter for movies and video games. His film *Soft for Digging* was an Official Selection of the Sundance Film Festival. He received a Game Developers Choice Award for his work on the bestselling video game Splinter Cell. JT lives in Brooklyn, New York. Visit his website at www.pettyofficial.com.

DAVID MICHAEL FRIEND is a freelance illustrator and animator living in Brooklyn, New York, whose creations have been used by such companies as Sesame Workshop, Disney, Jim Henson Company, and Cartoon Network. He illustrated J.T. Petty's *The Squampkin Patch*, *Blueberry Mouse* by Alice Low, and the graphic novel *Daniel and the Great Bearded One* by Richard W. Friend III. Visit him at www.dmfriend.com.